Praise fo

"The Weird Girls is an amazing prequel to a new ~~series~~. This new and upcoming author knows how to deliver suspense, humor, action and it's a surprise that she is just coming out with a novella/novel now. Mark my words, Ms. Robson will make her name known in no time with this great UF series."
- Under the Covers Book Blog

"The Weird Girls is a fantastic introduction to the Wird sister's world. The story takes off into an action-packed thrill ride from the first few pages and never stops. The characters are well developed for a novella and the world building is creative...If you're looking for a unique blend of the supernatural, magic, humor and girl power...look no further, the Wird sisters deliver!"
- Romancing the Dark Side

"Loved it! The women are entertaining & strong. You feel that connection between the sisters. This author shows me her series will be fun & eventful. Well worth reading before you pick up book 1 Sealed with a Curse."
– Angel's Guilty Pleasure

"This is a wonderfully imaginative, action packed story that sets up what looks to be a great new urban fantasy series by debut author, Cecy Robson...Robson writes with a sense of exuberance. I feel like she had as much fun writing The Weird Girls as I had reading it." **- She Wolf Reads**

"I like the trials that Celia had to go through, they were insane, and I was sitting on the edge of my seat wondering what was going to happen next." **- Urban Fantasy Reviews**

"Page after page it's packed with non-stop action, a lot of conflicts and well-developed characters. The Weird Girls is fast paced read, one I can guarantee you won't be able to put it down." - *The Bookaholic Cat*

"This was a strong introduction to what promises to be a great urban fantasy series. I'm getting hard to please when it comes to urban fantasy lately, but this hit all the write notes for me." - *My Bookish Ways*

"Considering this is a novella, not a full-length novel, Cecy Robson managed to create an action-packed story that left me excited to see what will happen next in Sealed with a Curse. If you're looking for a new urban fantasy series with a group of strong female heroines then I don't think you can go far wrong with this one." - *Feeling Fictional*

"The world building was fantastic. For a novella, we aren't bogged down with too much information. We get just enough mixed in with the fantastic plot to keep you turning the page eagerly in anticipation of what's to come... I am a fan for life now and I CANNOT WAIT to read *Sealed With A Curse*! If this novella knocked my socks off, the first full length in the series is bound to kick major ass!"
- *Sinfully Delicious Books*

"This was so much longer than I was expecting and it was good. I mean, REALLY good. It was almost as good as the actual book, itself...I loved every moment."
- *Book Marks the Spot*

"This novella was a welcome intro into the world of the Wird Sisters and I loved it. I highly recommend this nice and sweet novella to others. Go pick up your copy because you will not be disappointed." - *Doctor's Notes*

"I really liked this little introduction to the Weird Girls. I can't wait to read the next book in this series, *Sealed With A Curse*." *- Moonlight Reads*

The Carolina Beach Novels
Inseverable
Eternal
Infinite

APPS
Find Cecy on *Hooked – Chat stories APP* writing as
Rosalina San Tiago
Coming soon: *Crazy Maple's Chapters: Interactive Stories APP:* The Shattered Past and Weird Girls Series

A WEIRD GIRLS NOVELLA

CECY ROBSON

Copyright ©2012 Cecy Robson
Cover design © Kristin Clifton, Sweet Bird Designs
Formatting by BippityBoppityBook.com

Excerpt from Sealed with a Curse by Cecy Robson, copyright © 2012 by Cecy Robson

This book contains an excerpt from Sealed with a Curse by Cecy Robson, the first full length novel in The Weird Girls Urban Fantasy Romance series by Cecy Robson.

Published in the United States by Cecy Robson, L.L.C.

Print ISBN: 978-1-947330-17-7

Dear Reader,

The night I was born, a bat swept down in front of my father as he ran along a cobblestone road. My father ignored the bat in his haste to reach the Central American hospital where my mother labored with me. The bat disappeared in the shadows. In its place emerged a man, his dark skin bare, his voice ominous, his imposing form blocking my father's path. "Be wary of this one," he warned in Spanish. "She's not like the others."

Okay, I'll confess. This didn't happen. But it sounds way cooler than simply admitting my father used to kiss me goodnight wearing vampire fangs, and that he was the first person to trigger my overactive imagination.

I've always loved telling stories and getting a laugh. I've also enjoyed hearing stories, especially of the paranormal variety. Being of Latin descent, I heard many tales of spirits who haunt the night, of death lurking in the darkness waiting to claim her victims, and of circumstances which could only be explained by magic and creatures not of this earth.

The stories frightened me. I often slept clutching a crucifix while my plastic glow-in-the-dark Virgin Mary stood guard on my nightstand. And still I begged for more.

Sometimes the beasties of the night bumped too hard, and I swear I could see ghosts floating above me. I trekked on despite my fear, surviving each night while my plastic protector looked on.

On May 1, 2009, I decided to write a story about four unique women who must trek through their own darkness where supernasties bump hard, and bite harder. *The Weird Girls* series is the journey of Celia, Taran, Shayna, and Emme Wird, sisters who obtained their powers as a result of a backfired curse placed upon their Latina mother for marrying outside her race. Their story begins when the supernatural community of Lake Tahoe becomes aware of who they are, and what they can do.

"Weird" isn't welcomed among humans, nor is it embraced by those who hunt with fangs and claws, who cast magic in lethal blows, and who feast on others to survive. I wanted to show "weird" could be strong, brave, funny, and beautiful.

My "weird" girls will often face great terror, just like my seven-year-old frightened self, except without a glow-in-the-dark icon to keep them safe. Despite their fears, they fight like their lives depend on it, with only each other to rely on.

Sometimes, the darkness will devour the sisters. And sometimes, good won't succeed in kicking evil's ass. But just like glow-light Mary, there is hope. And there is humor—often twisted, a little inappropriate, and always hilarious—very much like a father saying goodnight to his children wearing a rubber ghoul mask and owning a collection of fake fangs no adult male should possess.

So, read on and check out my *Weird Girls* series. Maybe you'll find I'm really "not like the others."

Salud!

Cecy

ACKNOWLEDGMENTS

There are two people who I wouldn't be here without: my agent, Nicole Resciniti, and my husband, Jamie. Nicole works to make my writing dreams a reality. Jamie believed in me from the very first pages I typed. I'm so blessed to have them in my life.

Chapter One

The music pounded hard enough to shake Emme's fuzzy navel, the umbrella in Shayna's piña colada, Taran's martini, and my Corona. I'd shoved pieces of cocktail napkin into my über sensitive ears the moment we sat. But I wasn't going to complain about the eardrum-busting music or the crowd of young men sitting across from us ogling my sisters. We were there to celebrate.

Two years had passed since we'd left our native New Jersey. Two years of roaming the States as travelling nurses. Two years of searching for a place to settle down. We'd stumbled into the Lake Tahoe region when our agency transferred us to a local hospital on temporary assignment. We'd thought it would be fun to check out the area. We hadn't expected to fall in love with the lush forests, the breathtaking mountains, or the mysticism of the lake. But we had, and collectively agreed to make it our home sweet home.

Shayna raised her girly drink; her blue eyes and grin sparkled despite the dimness in the booth. "To the Wird Girls finding an awesome place to live," she hiccuped.

"To a thirty-year mortgage and a shitload of

remodeling," Taran muttered. She tried to complain, but couldn't hide that siren grin that made males trip over their erections. She was happy to settle down, and she damn well knew it.

"To beautiful Lake Tahoe," Emme added almost silently. She blushed when I glanced her way. I'd like to say she was just tipsy, but no. Emme blushed as easily as the wind blew fireflies. "W-well it is beautiful here, Celia."

"I know, sweetie." I tapped my bottle against her frou-frou drink. "Salud."

I polished off my beer. It was my sixth round, still no buzz. Then again I could chug a keg. Alcohol had no effect on me. My lightweight sisters slurred their words after three. In their defense, they didn't have an inner beast with the metabolism of four linebackers to help them out. The waitress rushed over and slapped another Corona down before I could ask and hurried off. I snagged it before it tipped over. Ordinarily one might think of her as a diligent, fast, hardworking, go-getter—nah, she was just scared I'd eat her. Humans never knew what we were, yet they perceived we weren't anything like them. They didn't need the amplified senses of preternaturals to know we were different. Problem was, different didn't appeal to most. And "weird" just plain terrified.

"Oh my goodness," Emme said. "You didn't even peek her way or anything."

My sisters had definitely received the less-daunting side of our backfired curse. I pushed my long hair from my face and shrugged. After years of being feared, I was almost used to it. Almost. "I don't think tigers have to necessarily look at their prey to scare them."

Emme placed a gentle hand on my shoulder. The jarring club lights further lightened her fair skin and blond hair and bleached out most of her freckles. "It's not you, Celia. It's these silly humans who never want to give you a chance. You're *beautiful*. And so is your inner golden tigress."

Taran rolled her huge blue eyes. "Tigers *are* beautiful, Emme. But most people aren't stupid enough to pet one." She sipped her martini as she gave me the once-over. "Or piss one off."

Or date one, I thought to myself, taking in the frat boys on spring break continuing to stare and whisper about my sisters.

"Adriana Lima is mine," one said of Taran.

"I'll take the blonde," the other murmured.

"I'll go with the cute brunette with the ponytail."

"Hey, I called dibs on her first," his friend complained.

There were four of them. Four of us. One of the guys fighting over Shayna had taken an interest in me. That is, until he looked at me. *Really* looked at me. He smiled, but his scent of anticipation and lust quickly evaporated, replaced by the aroma of fear. He'd seen beyond my green eyes, olive skin, and long wavy hair to spot the predator lurking within. He saw her ready to pounce, ready to shred, ready to kill. Beautiful or not, tigers had that effect on humans.

Taran shimmied out of the booth. An impressive feat in the tiny, curve-hugging yellow dress she wore. If the hem lay an inch shorter, she'd end up on the Internet. "Shit. I have to pee."

Shayna grinned at Taran as she ambled out, her eyes alternating from sparkly to glassy. So not a good sign. "I think that's an oxymoron, dude." She threw in a giggle, just to further clarify she was snockered.

I shook my head. Emme smiled softly. "I'll go with Taran." Emme was only five feet tall, and just shy of a hundred pounds soaking wet and bloated. Taran, although only three inches taller, towered over her in those stepladders she affectionatcly referred to as "shoes." Me? Nothing said comfy like jeans, Uggs, and a long-sleeved tee.

The minute they disappeared into the hall leading to the ladies room, one of the good ol' frat boys approached Shayna, careful to avoid eye contact with me. "Hey, hot stuff. How about a dance?"

Shayna's glee faded when she realized I'd be alone if she went to dance. I smiled as best I could without scaring her potential date for the evening. "It's okay. I'll just hang and wait for Emme. Go on," I urged when she hesitated.

The guy snaked his arm around Shayna and led her onto the dance floor. Her sleek black ponytail whipped behind her as she shot me one more tentative glance. She watched me for a while. At first I thought she might return to hang with her spinster-in-the-making sister until the call of Beyoncé loosened the hesitant muscles of her slender frame. It didn't take long for Shayna to move like the world's happiness depended on her booty shakes. It did, however, take a hell of a long time for Emme and Taran to return from the bathroom. The waitress dropped my eighth beer down just as I spotted Emme's hands waving madly amidst the crowd forming near the ladies' room. "Celia! Ceeeeeelia!"

What the hell?

I slipped out of the booth and rushed toward the crowd. The throng of horny and drunken patrons parted as I stalked, my hips swinging like a predator staking out her turf. *That's right. Stay back. Scary female approaching.*

As I reached Emme, a deep buzzing sound vibrated from the bathroom, followed by a high-pitched squeal, topped off by Taran's oh-so colorful language. I half-groaned, half-growled. *Crap. How much trouble can someone get into in the bathroom?*

I froze. Apparently a lot.

A fiery redhead stomped out of the restroom smelling like burnt toast, sporting a spiky new hairdo most porcupines would envy. I swore under my breath. Taran must have struck her with a mini-bolt of lightning. Her tresses stood out like wires, and the singed tips smoked. And God only knew what Taran had done to the rest of her dress. Scorched pieces of fabric barely covered Red's pricey and fricasseed bra.

Her crazed eyes scanned the crowd. "Who's with the slutty brunette?"

Emme glanced my way before raising a cautious hand. "Sh-sh-she's my sister."

The redhead stormed to Emme and jabbed an irate finger in her face. "Your sister's a *bitch*."

Maybe. But Emme certainly wasn't. I shoved my way between them. "Leave her alone, and get out of our way." My raspy voice remained deceptively calm. Yet Red easily picked up on my underlying threat: Mess with her, mess with me.

Red's finger slowly lowered and her jaw slackened. She stumbled back, tripping over her feet and shoving her way through the crowd and out the exit. The ladies in line quickly followed suit and gave us ample room to pass. Perhaps there was a nice fir tree they could use out back. Emme stayed close to my heels as I shoved opened the door to the bathroom, her meek little voice shaking. "Should I get Shayna?"

"No, I think—"

My first clue should have been that Taran's swear words had stopped bouncing off the stark white tiles like ping-pong balls. My second? The waft of dry herbs that filtered into my nose and screamed a warning. *Witch.* Witch magic. Taran was going head-to-head with an official worship-the-earth-talisman-wearing-broom-humper extraordinaire.

Taran's blue irises blanched to crystal from the gamut of power tingling around a sandy-haired witch's aura. "Sandy" smiled though it lacked any hint of warmth,

5

friendliness, or love. In fact, if she was going for, "I'll skin you alive and use your flesh as bedroom slippers," one might say she pulled it off.

"*Silentio. Non vide*," Sandy muttered, all the while smiling and calling forth her bladder-releasing power.

Knowing Spanish helped me translate the Latin words. *Silence and . . . don't look?*

Every muscle and tendon in my body tightened. She'd cast a spell to conceal any sounds and images from the club patrons. *Jesus, what did she plan to do?*

The aroma of crushed thyme thickened the air as her spell accelerated, coating my taste buds with a hint of her power. Yup, definitely not a good sign. My inner tigress circled restlessly, pawing at my ribcage with her claws, demanding out. "Taran," I warned, "time to go home."

Taran met the witch's smile with one that sent Emme running, hopefully to get Shayna, the car, or both. The heavy door swung shut behind Emme. A loud click told me Sandy locked us in, and anyone who could possibly help us out. Sparks sizzled from the tips of Taran's elegantly manicured hands as she gathered her magic. "No worries, Ceel. This will only take a minute."

"*Taran*," I warned again. My fangs protruded without my consent. Another sign proclaiming deep shittiness awaited.

The sparks magnified into mini bolts of lightning as Taran stretched out her fingers. A small funnel of wind gathered around Sandy, sending bits of abandoned toilet paper circling around her. The fluorescent lights hummed and flickered just before everything went black.

"Taran!"

I tackled Taran into the handicapped stall as the equivalent of a supernatural cherry bomb took out the wall instead of my sister. The hole, roughly the size of our new dining room table, gave a great view of the dance floor where Shayna continued to shake her tiny, yet obviously shimmy-able butt. The crowd of onlookers had returned to their drunken debauchery, swallowing poor Emme as she jumped up and down trying futilely to get Mini-Shakira's attention. It might have been funny, had I not feared we were finally about to die that miserable death we'd spent a lifetime avoiding.

Taran rubbed her head. "Son of a *bitch*."

A deep growl thundered in my chest. My tigress' eyes replaced my own and locked on the witch's feet. She casually walked across the checkered floor, her red stilettos clicking like the pendulum of a grandfather clock, *tick-tock, tick-tock, tick-tock.*

She reeled into the black stall where we lay. Time was up.

For her.

"Well, well—"

I kicked the door right in her face.

She flew backwards into the sink and smashed her head into the mirror. Sometimes, I couldn't control my strength. Fear of dying in a public bathroom will do that to a gal. I hauled Taran up by her elbow while her latest fan seemed down for the count. The cracks in the mirror spiderwebbed from her bleeding skull. I secretly hoped that since it was technically her head that broke the mirror, the bad luck fell on her.

When Sandy lurched from the sink and a second, equally pissed-off version of herself appeared to block the door leading out, I knew I was very much mistaken. Taran's head whipped back and forth between them. "It's the same person," I snarled. She smelled the same, looked the same, and also bled from her forehead the same way. The only difference was she'd divided her magic in two.

Taran gathered her power once more. "I'll take the bitch at the door. You take the bitch at the sink."

Sandy—both of them—surprised me by laughing. "*Mures*," they both spat.

That one pretty much got lost in translation. I prowled toward her. My claws shot from my fingers like bullets from a chamber. She didn't move. She didn't gather her magic. She didn't blink. She simply laughed. Either she'd hit her head a little too hard or she didn't fear us. The latter scared the hell out of me. My beast remained sure we could take her. My human half knew something sinister lurked beneath, bubbling with a touch of dark and a spoonful of evil.

A transparent heaviness filled the air, reeking of garbage and festering meat. The ten plastic soap dispensers lining the wall of the mammoth counter exploded one by one, like a row of bottles being shot to bits. Paper towels fluttered in the air around us like birds. The pipes beneath us clanged and a toilet flushed for no reason.

I hated when my human side was right.

I heard the first squeak and the scratch of tiny clawed feet followed by a few more. A lot more. Taran heard it, too. In her panic, she blasted a bolt of lightning into her psycho witch, taking out the obviously evil tampon dispenser in the far wall. Chunks of cardboard and cotton pelted me in the hair and back, and still I heard the squeaks getting louder, getting closer, getting *scurrier*.

The Sandy Taran attempted to fight had somehow appeared on the sink next to her other half. She sat on the counter with her legs crossed, swinging them merrily as the result of her enchantment reached a creepy crescendo.

The large brass drain near the sinks began to stir. "Taran. We need to get out of here."

"Damn it, Celia—"

I clutched her arm when the brass drain tipped and a pink whiskered nose poked through. *Mures. . . . Rats.*

Chapter Two

One rat, two rats, three—*oh, crap*. I slammed my protective shields around me before the creatures could send me into a full-grown seizure. Animals and I, well, let's just say we mixed a little too well. They'd touch me. I'd turn into them. It wasn't pretty. It wasn't welcome. And it typically took me hours to days to return to my human form.

I shoved us back as a swarm of black, white, brown, and red vermin spilled from the drain as if rammed forward, squeaking and snapping their tiny fangs. They swept over the tile in a wave of fur. Taran screamed. I kicked the first few that leapt onto my legs, sending their bodies to crunch into the walls as Taran let loose her lightning. Their small creepy bodies slid down the tiled walls, leaving splotches of red. I believed them dead . . . until they joined to form several more versions of Sandy—bleeding from identical gashes on their heads and cackling. Let's not forget the cackling. It wouldn't be the same without the cackling.

My head whipped toward the original Sandy versions near the sink. The fuzzy critters hung from them like live coats of fur, their little naked tails flicking with delight.

That's when I knew she was messing with us. Real rats or not, to some extent the spell targeted fear and created an illusion.

Emme and Shayna's screams announced their arrival just as the overhead vent flung open and I was showered with tiny claws and warm fur. I wrenched them off me, feeling my skin crawl, panic pounding my heart like an axe. Behind me, Shayna grabbed the remains of the metal tampon dispenser. As the lights flickered back on, Shayna released the magnitude of her gift, transforming the warped metal into two deadly machetes. She grunted and swung her thin arms, hacking into the tiny fuzzy bodies while the witches' laughter escalated with glee.

Emme stood on the toilet seat, pushing back the rats with her telekinetic *force*. She shook violently, managing to keep her concentration until more rats swam up from the toilet bowl and spilled out between her legs. A white rat drenched with water scurried up her leg. She jerked hard, flinging it into the air and toward Shayna's blade. Shayna severed the mini-beast in two, splashing me with its warm blood.

Someone pounded on the door. "Ladies. Open the door. You're not allowed to lock that shit up."

I wasn't a screamer. But I almost screamed then. Three versions of Sandy circled me, tossing armfuls of their little friends at me like confetti. I swatted one away into Shayna. It fastened onto her ponytail and found a way into her tunic. She shrieked and fell against the wall, mashing the rat against her back.

Shayna's blue eyes widened and her skin paled as the horde crawled over her thin frame, enveloping her like a blanket. I kicked my way through the now knee-deep floor of flicking tails and ripped them off her. The witches' manic laugh spilled into my ears, making it hard to keep my focus. But I supposed that was the point.

"You need to get the hell out. There's a line." The man pounded harder and his voice boomed. "Open the damn door!"

Shayna screamed, uncertain whether my claws or the rats raked against her skin. My eyes scanned the laughing witches. There were six now, all laughing, all spinning, all covered with rodents. All resembled each other. Except one. The talisman of the one furthest to my right flickered. She was the one I needed to stop.

I whispered into Shayna's ear as tiny teeth cut through my shirt and legs wrangled their way into my hair. "The witch at three o'clock. Do you see her?"

Shayna didn't respond. I shook her hard and swatted away a few more rats crawling against her neck. She nodded. "We take her talisman and this goes away."

I'm not sure if she heard me over Emme's screams for me or Taran's swearing, but I left her and lurched forward.

Someone rammed full force into the door. A three-hundred pound bouncer barreled his way in. "The fuck!" he hollered, his voice sounding more like a Girl Scout selling cookies than a big, hulking male. The rats snaked around his limbs like ribbons. His lids peeled back, and his head jerked in horrified disbelief.

The horde spilled out into the hall and into the club. The shrieks informed me Sandy's silencing spell and camouflage screen hadn't carried past the bathroom. The bouncer screamed, falling into a live bed of flea-infested fur.

Emme's cries bordered on hysteria. She stood on pipes anchored into the wall. "Celia! Celia! Celia!" she sobbed.

That's when my tigress had enough. The terror searing my brain stood no chance against my anger and need to protect. I leapt across the floor of tiny scampering bodies, *changing* as my arms and legs stretched out. My clothes and shoes shredded and fell from my body as my four-hundred pound tigress emerged.

The witch stopped laughing then. In fact, it was her turn to scream. My roars forced her into a stall. I tackled her into the floor, ignoring the angry balls of fur that leapt on my back and punctured their teeth into my hide.

My fangs bit into her talisman and yanked it off with one hard pull. The witch screamed and snatched wildly at the chain hanging from my maw. It had little effect. Her magic was strong, but her physical strength was no match against mine.

The rats vanished one by one in poofs of yellow dandelion dust. I backed away from the witch, her expression both furious and panicked. "Give me back my power," she hissed. "Give it back to me now!"

The witch lunged at me, only to freeze as the tip of Shayna's machete angled against her throat. "Don't move, dude." Shayna's voice shook with leftover fear, but her tone made it clear her typical cheerleader persona wouldn't stop her from slicing the witch's head off.

I *changed* as I stood, dropping the heavy gold necklace with the green stone into my human hands. My sisters gathered around me. The bouncer lay on the floor convulsing, the whites of his eyes bleached under the light.

"Taran, would you do the honors?" I asked.

Taran's smile returned once more. "Hell, yeah."

I threw the talisman in the air. The restroom charged with Taran's magic as she released a blue and white spray of fire dead center into the stone. It hovered in the air and flickered. The witch charged. I crouched, thinking she'd attack. She didn't. Instead she hauled ass through the large hole in the wall and kept going, across the now-empty club and in the direction of the exit. Rats, freaky diseased-coated rats. Now *there* was an original way to clear a dance floor. I didn't complain, though. The humans were safe and out of harm's way.

Taran angled her head to look through the hole. "Damn. Why did she—"

The talisman sparkled above us and spun, breaking apart into large shards. The chunks imbedded into the ceiling and began to blink, slowly at first like soft, twinkling Christmas lights, then faster and faster, similar to a Vegas sign. No, not like a Vegas sign. More like a—

Every hair on my body saluted our impending doom. Oh, *shit*. "Bomb!"

"Wh-what?" Emme stammered.

I tackled my sisters, slamming us on top of the bouncer. I *shifted* us into the basement as the club exploded above. The ceiling caved in a landslide of rubble. I *shifted* us again through the foundation, breaking up our bodies into particles so minute we passed through the cement and dirt as easy as sand through a colander. Cool ability, huh? No. Not so much. I couldn't see, couldn't breathe, when I *shifted*. Neither could anyone else. Any wrong movement and I could resurface in Lake Tahoe and drown us.

Luck and I weren't the best of friends. But this time she cut me a break. By some miracle to end all miracles I resurfaced behind the club in a small grassy section overlooking the lake. My sisters gagged and choked, gasping for much-needed oxygen. I slumped naked over the bouncer with my head spinning, trying hard not to throw up on his "Tahoe Babes Like It on Top" T-shirt. I'd never *shifted* that many people before. My spinning vision and pounding head told me I never should again.

I clutched the bouncer, trying to stay warm as the cold February breeze rushed against my back and flung my hair in all directions. For the first time in years, I could say I got naked and horizontal with someone. Although I wished I knew his name, and that it had meant something, and that it didn't have to involve an army of rats.

The world spun in a blur of red and black. When the nausea-inducing teacup ride I'd forced my body into ground to a halt, I realized the club had transformed into a literal inferno. The loud blasting of a fire truck horn forced me to a kneeling position. Police officers shoved club patrons back as the spray from several hoses tackled the flames lifting into the skies. My shoulders slumped with relief. Thank God the rats had scared the clubbers out.

"We have to get the hell out of here," Taran spat. She shook my shoulder as she stood. "Celia. *Ceel*, are you okay?"

I nodded and stumbled to my feet. The bouncer remained out cold. Being engulfed by a horde of vermin in the ladies room could have had something to do with it. I remained very naked. And while I'd never stolen anything, I reasoned that saving this poor sap's life made it okay to commandeer his obnoxious T-shirt. I grabbed the edges of his shirt and yanked. The collar had just slipped over his head when he snapped to attention. His eyes widened. Since he was a good-looking fellow, despite his lack of neck, his shock caught me off guard. Surely this wasn't the first time he'd woken next to a naked female.

He tore away from me with a backwards crab-spotting-a-pelican move. "What are you doing?"

"Um."

"What the *hell* are you doing?"

I was known for my muscle, not my flair. I shoved his shirt over my head while he gripped his man-boobs like they might fall off. Then I ran. Fast, like I-just-fought-off-a-witch-and-set-a-building-on-fire fast. The pebbles littering the path cut into my feet. But the bouncer's birdlike screams pushed me forward. Despite my long lean muscles and tight abdominals, being naked in front of a total stranger was not my thing. Neither was obliterating private property.

My sisters chased me. Taran swore behind me. Emme and Shayna begged me to slow down. I didn't until I reached our Subaru Legacy. Dammit, this was supposed to be a night of celebration, not getting into a smack-down in the restroom with a psycho witch and her freak-ass minions.

Emme wheezed and sputtered as she key-fobbed the door. She handed me the keys and we quickly scrambled inside. I floored it out of the parking lot of the former Club Ooo-La-La just as an ambulance screeched past us.

"Okay. That sucked," Taran muttered.

Shayna whipped her head behind to watch the ensuing chaos. "Dude! We like . . . *demolished* a building."

I could understand Shayna's fear. Destroying a building was just plain nutso and irresponsible. We'd never even littered.

I swerved onto Route 80, my foot stomping on the gas. Once more, the lake came into view. I lowered my window and tried to take a few breaths to allow the mysticism of the water to settle my beast. Shayna's face remained glued to the rear window. "Good Lord. Do you think we'll have to pay for that?"

Taran crossed her arms. "We're not paying for shit. They started it."

"I'm sure they have insurance, Shayna." I glanced over at Taran. "What happened, anyway?"

Taran shrugged. "The redhead tried to take my paper towel. I wouldn't let her."

"What?" I asked, certain I'd misheard.

"I reached for the towel and she yanked it out of my hands. I yanked it back and then she splashed my dress with water."

Shock and humiliation left me as Taran's words sunk in. I made a sharp turn off the road and into the beach parking lot. In the night, the lake appeared navy blue instead of crystal clear. I focused on how the waves licked against the large boulders at the edge and how the sound was more song than noise. Still, it did nothing to soothe me. I clenched my jaw and turned to face Taran. "Tell me you're joking."

Taran frowned. "What do you mean?"

My body shook with the need to rip the dashboard off and beat Taran with it. "Tell me we didn't just take out an entire nightclub over a freaking paper towel!"

Taran narrowed her eyes. "I told you, she splashed water on me, too. I zapped her for being a bitch and then her stupid friend got involved." She huffed. "I didn't initially realize her friend was a witch. But even if I had, I couldn't let her do that to me, Celia."

The steering wheel dented beneath my grip. "I don't *believe* you, Taran!"

"Celia—"

I veered toward her. "Don't you dare try to justify what we did back there by—"

"Th-they were making fun of me," Emme said almost quietly.

Taran's head shot toward the back. "Emme, don't."

I looked to Shayna, who frowned and shook her head, confused. Anger stomped out my remaining patience. "*What?*"

"Nothing," Taran snapped. "I told you—"

I held out my hand to silence her. "What happened, Emme?" I asked a little more calmly.

Emme stared down at her small hands. "They were drunk and practically fell out of the stalls. The one with the red hair paused when she caught sight of me. She scowled, like I'd done something to bother her." Emme sighed. "She staggered toward me and poked me in the arm like I couldn't possibly be real. 'What the hell are you?' she asked. Even in her state she knew I was . . . different. I didn't answer her and tried to ignore her. She asked me again. When I wouldn't respond she called me a freak and backed away. Her friend—the witch—was fixing her hair at the mirror. The redhead whispered something to her, and pointed at me. That's when they both started taunting me."

"They more than taunted her, Celia." Taran's face hardened. "And they called her worse than a freak."

Emme's hand cupped Taran's shoulder. "It's okay."

Taran ripped her hand away. "It's not okay, Emme." Her gaze traveled around us. "Everyone recognizes we're not like them, but those bitches seemed to think they had a free pass to say anything they wanted. When I stepped out of the stall I told them to shut the hell up. They quieted for a moment before they started in on me. I told them to fuck off, and they did. But when I reached for the towel, the redhead snatched it out of my grasp." Bitter tears leaked out of my tough-as-sin sister. "I won't put up with the shit we dealt with in school, Ceel. I won't. And I'll be damned if I let anyone mistreat Emme."

Shayna crossed her arms around herself protectively. She leaned back into the seat to stare out at the water, no doubt thinking about the cruelty we'd been forced to endure in our childhood and how it always managed to find its way into our adult lives. Emme had returned to analyzing the creases of her small palms. Taran just fumed, hard enough for a spark of blue and white to sizzle above her dark hair. I paused, taking a moment to settle my beast and the whirlwind of emotions spinning my insides. "Why didn't you tell me? Why did you let me believe it was all about the damn paper towel?"

"I didn't think you needed reminding what freaks we all are." Taran gave me a one-shoulder shrug. "Especially seeing how you've had a harder time than the rest of us."

Harder time? I guess she had a point. I was nine when our parents were killed—too young to take on the parental role suddenly thrust into my arms. And yet I had.

Although we were all born "different," my sisters' powers didn't manifest until puberty. I'd obtained added strength and my first *change* at age eight. Looking back, it was probably God's way of assigning me as their protector.

17

After all, the spell our wicked aunt cast upon our mother for marrying outside her race condemned our parents with short lives—a curse which came to fruition the night our home was burglarized. The other part of the curse? The one meant to damn any child conceived from their union with sickness and frailty? That one somehow backfired and made us strong, and so unique; nothing like us existed on earth.

I covered my face with my hands trying to push away the memories of our parent's deaths . . . and everything that followed their passing.

I'm not sure how many more breaths I took before I could angle the car back onto the road. I barely saw the street, the lake, the wall of thick pines hugging the edge of the road, or the lights of the oncoming cars. All that clouded my vision were the nameless faces of the kids who had been mean to us. With the exception of our parents, then our foster mother, the adults we'd encountered hadn't been any nicer. Taran was right, we were freaks . . . ones who had never fit in. And having a last name like Wird gave others the pleasure of nicknaming us the "weird girls". The moniker followed us no matter where we ended up. I hated school, and spent most of my afternoons in detention for fighting those who targeted my sisters. Funny how in some ways I remained that kid in detention, seething and exhausted, knowing another day of trouble lay ahead with no end in sight.

None of us spoke the rest of the way to our new home in Dollar Point. I pulled into the driveway and stared at the beautiful blue custom Colonial. We thought we'd finally found a home where we could be safe. Had we been fools to believe it?

I cut the engine. No one moved or made an effort to get out. In the silence, a multitude of worst-case scenarios played like a movie trailer in my mind. Taran twisted her body to face me. "You would have done the same, Celia," she said. Her voice grew more and more defensive. "And you damn well know it."

"Maybe," I said. "But there's one difference."

Taran glared. "Oh, yeah? And what's that?"

I met Taran's stare. Although she knew I'd never hurt her, she still feared the power of my beast. She dropped her gaze but not her attitude. I sighed. "Because in high school, the homecoming queen would have retaliated with snide remarks, not magic. You pissed off a witch, Taran. That means her entire coven will come after us."

Chapter Three

My bare feet padded along the cold driveway. I adjusted my thick white cotton robe before bending over and retrieving the morning paper. Right smack on the front page was a picture highlighting our oh-so-thrilling night. The hellish inferno, a.k.a. Club Ooo-La-La, sat larger than life before my bloodshot eyes. I groaned, convinced the flames resembled one giant middle finger "F-You" tribute to the Wird girls. My stomach churned as I read on. Patrons credited the neckless bouncer with saving the day. He'd been the last one to leave after ensuring everyone had exited, one party-hopper stated. He'd even admitted to trying to bat out the flames with his shirt. *Yeah, right. I guess he had to explain his last-minute appearance and missing shirt.*

Rats chewing on gas lines were blamed, leaving us thankfully free of the much anticipated arson charge. I threw out the paper almost immediately, grateful our mug shots hadn't made the front cover.

Emme handed me a plate of food, piled high with eggs and sausage. I barely ate. Our lack of prison time, while comforting, did little to ease my retaliation worries.

The witches would find us. Covens were a lot like tight-knit families. Take on one, take on the entire spell-wielding cheer squad. I could relate. Still, that didn't mean I looked forward to the showdown.

"Did you notice anything different?" Shayna asked. Four knives the length of chair legs sat tucked into the leather belt fastened around her nightie. She usually slept with a knife under her pillow, but the mercenary-for-hire getup was excessive, even for her. Thankfully, we'd learned long ago to knock before disturbing her sleep.

"No. Nothing at all."

Taran sipped her tea. "Well, maybe those wenches realize we're not going to take their shit."

Emme shot me an optimistic glance. I didn't comment, refusing to give them false hope. Taran knew the witches wouldn't back down. Her attempt was made to ease our sisters' fears. But as much as I hated them being on edge, the tension would keep their guard up, and hopefully keep them safe.

I retreated to my bedroom, my brain muddled with how to handle the witches and their flying monkeys of doom. Beings of magic guarded their proprietary secrets carefully. It's not like a "Wicked Spell-Casters R Us" website awaited us with answers. Who could I call? Danny, my dear friend and genius extraordinaire, had become enthralled by the supernatural world after I helped protect him and his father against Mafioso-like vampires years ago. Since then, he'd researched the mystical world just for fun, shocking the bejeebers out of me. Personally, I thought he'd take up knitting a strait jacket after that nightmare experience. If anything, his near-death experience fueled his curiosity about the superbeasties and what made them go bump in the night.

Danny and I had dated briefly as teens. He'd ended our relationship just before he left Jersey for Stanford, claiming he wasn't what I needed. It took me a long time to understand what he'd meant, and even longer to admit he'd been right. We'd stayed in touch because aside from my sisters, he'd been my one true friend, and one I could trust with our lives.

My sisters and I, while technically supernatural, didn't fall under any mystical category. Therefore, we didn't quite belong... *anywhere*. And although mortal, once the backfired curse kicked in, we no longer thought of ourselves as fully human. We resigned to fly under the radar, as much as our uniqueness would allow. And even though Danny was human, he knew more than us and was frequently our go-to guy when we had questions about the world we'd done our best to avoid. I called him so he could ease my fears, tell me my concerns were ridiculous, accuse me of being neurotic.

Danny answered my call on the second ring. It surprised me given he was immersed in his doctoral studies at Stanford. "Hey, Celia! How's it going, pretty girl?"

"Taran picked a fight with a witch last night in a public bathroom. We destroyed her talisman and burned down the building. I think her coven plans to retaliate and turn us into gophers... or kill us. One of the two, for sure."

A long, long pause was followed by: "*Holy crap.* Celia, you have to get out of there!"

So much for easing my worries. "We can't, Danny. This is home now." I stood and paced my bedroom suite, spilling the details of our rip-roaring night. "What can we expect?"

"Hang on." Fumbling ensued on the other end followed by what sounded like books falling from high places and pages flipping open. "According to *The Brown Book of Magic*, in destroying the witch's talisman, you've cut her power by half."

"Oh, well, that's good."

The pause on the other end told me I was very much

mistaken. "Ah, Celia, witches are born with magic in them."

"I know, Danny. That's what differentiates them from humans."

More pausing. More trouble, I presumed. "They spend their lives building their magic into their talismans—staffs, rings, necklaces, etc., to amplify the magic they're born with. Apparently it's a lot of work and takes years of grueling effort."

I stopped pacing. "Um. Okay. So what does that mean?"

"Ah, well, you basically stripped her of her position and she will likely never regain the power she's lost. It's the equivalent of a general being reduced to private status."

"Well, that's not too bad—"

"After he's publicly whipped before the entire army."

"Um, no one saw—"

"And peed on by feral dogs."

It was my turn to pause. "So, there's nothing we can do. Her coven *will* come after us?"

Danny's shaky breath answered for him. So did his ominous tone. "They'll basically form a circle around the witch who provoked you at the next gathering. She'll focus on yours or Taran's face. They'll call forth a location spell and find you to answer for the insult."

"But she came after us."

"Even if you could prove to the head witch she started the trouble, it would likely only earn her a slap on the wrist. After all, she technically kept the fight shadowed from the patrons. And while that bouncer walked in on everything, she could have easily altered his memories with a simple spell." He flipped through more pages. "Hmm."

"Good hmm, or bad hmm?" He didn't answer. "Danny?"

"There is something that may protect your family,

but I'm not crazy about the idea."

"Like a weapon or something?"

"Uh, you can say that." More pages flipped. He groaned. "Yeah, really not crazy about this, Celia."

I tapped my fingers against my dresser. "Danny, they're my family. I have to do something."

"I know you do, Celia." He sighed. "Look, as head of the family, you can challenge their head witch to a duel. It's called 'invoking the Ninth Law'. Your sisters will be spared from any retaliation, whether you win or not."

A trickle of cold sweat found its way down my spine. I didn't want to have to kill . . . again. Danny must have sensed my fear. "No one has to die, Celia. It's more like whoever cries *misericordia* —or 'mercy'—first, loses. But keep in mind, as head witch, she'll be a lot stronger than the witch you faced."

I swore under my breath, thinking back to the rats. But what choice did I have? "I know, but—it's fine. I'll do it."

"I still think it's wiser to move."

My mind flashed with images of our house. We'd purchased it at auction. The previous owners had wrecked it—the carpet had been torn up, angry fists had punched through the sheetrock, and yellow paint had been splashed over the beautiful hardwood floors. Still, they hadn't robbed the 3,500-square-foot colonial of its heart. We had big plans to make it so warm, so endearing. I couldn't think to abandon something we'd yearned for all our lives. "We're not going anywhere, Danny."

I heard Danny shut the book and place it down. "Celia, please think this through. Just because the rules say no one has to die, that doesn't mean the head witch won't try to kill you."

Chapter Four

I didn't share my "duel until someone cries 'uncle'" conversation with my sisters. They'd go ape, and there was no sense in worrying them until I had to. So we waited for the witches to contact us. I expected something dramatic—a raven perhaps delivering the "I'll get you, my pretties, and your little dog, too," papers, or maybe something more technologically advanced like a curse via email. It seemed, though, even that was too much to hope for.

I ran along the snowy beach of Lake Tahoe, dressed in black spandex running pants with a matching long-sleeved top. The bitter morning wind slapped against my hot cheeks. Sweat trickled between my breasts. And my buttocks and thighs tightened like flesh-covered stone. It all felt so damn good, especially with the caress of Tahoe's magic encouraging me forward. The ten miles I'd run would have drained most. Instead it enlivened my spirit and made my tigress beg for more. If she couldn't fight, she needed to run, or else the predator would choose to hunt those who threatened the ones we loved.

My ears and senses remained vigilant, seeking out

any unusual scent, sound, or presence. Several days had passed without incident. We'd returned to our nursing jobs, grocery shopping, and laundry duties. And yet while no one mentioned it, we didn't exactly return to a sense of normalcy. I finished my run and cut through the snow-covered path back to our development. The firs and rhododendrons covered by a thick blanket of snow parted just a few yards away, revealing the house closest to the path. Our neighbors were virtually nonexistent, with the exception of one.

Mrs. Mancuso hadn't liked four young, single women moving in next door. The first day we'd moved in she banged on our door. Emme mistakenly thought some kind, neighborly soul had arrived to bring us 'Welcome to Tahoe' cookies. There were no cookies, just a whole lot of attitude and a great deal of neck skin.

"This is a family neighborhood," Mrs. Mancuso had huffed. "They'll be no whorin' under my watch."

"Who says we'll let you watch?" Taran shot back.

I hadn't realized women in their eighties flipped people off until then.

I ran up the small incline to the walkway, hoping to avoid yet another Mrs. Mancuso tongue-lashing. It seemed the grouchy old hag waited like a leopard behind her hummingbird-patterned curtains to pounce on the would-be Wird gazelles.

Typically I took this time to cool down and stretch. But the commotion before me had me bolting full speed.

"What the *hell* do you bitches want?"

Oh. No.

Taran stood on our large wooden porch with her hands on her hips, her jaw clenched tight, and her glare fixed on the coven of witches gathered on our front sidewalk. Shayna lingered next to her with her hands close to her daggers, her sharp blue eyes sweeping along the crowd of thirteen. Emme kept her hands clasped in front of her, anxious, but ready to defend her family.

Ambrosial scents of spearmint, sage, rosemary, and basil thickened the air surrounding our development. It might have been comforting had I not feared Taran's fire would ignite our visitors like marshmallows . . . and that they'd unleash a plague onto our house that would make leprosy seem like diaper rash.

The incident at the club hadn't been pretty. I didn't get the impression this would be all rainbows, puppies, and potpourri. Still, I didn't want the Hermione Granger wannabees to think they could push us around.

My eyes darted along our cul-de-sac and took in their cars. It seemed every witch owned a Jetta. And their collective magic rose like the sun against their auras.

The witch closest to me held the power of the heavens within her reach. At first glance, I would have mistaken her for a vampire. Her beauty rivaled theirs. Long ebony hair traveled in perfect waves along her bold red Renaissance dress. Her lithe body rested against our Subaru and she gripped the long wooden staff at her side. I took her to be the second in command. It was an easy guess, seeing how the head witch was the only other gal wearing a velvet maiden gown, and *her* power cracked like the power of hell's whips and thundered around her like the eye of a cyclone.

Their BFFs, conversely, dressed like they shopped at the Gap.

The dark-haired witch blinked her sapphire eyes my way before returning her attention to the mounting tension on my front porch. To her right, a young woman with dark spiky hair wrote feverishly on a scroll. "Sandy," the witch from the paper towel incident, hid behind a cluster of witches gathered in our driveway. At the sight of me, she sidled onto Mrs. Mancuso's property, tipping over one of the creepy lawn gnomes adorning the front lawn.

The head witch's tight, strawberry-blond curls

barely moved when a strong gust of wind billowed her green velvet skirt, revealing her bare feet and three toe rings on her left foot. Each silver loop held minute amethyst stones sizzling with a supersized amount of collective power. I couldn't see her face since she was currently going toe-to-toe with my scratch-your-eyes-out-first, ask-questions-later sister.

The coven parted as I stalked my way through the crowd, much like the patrons had at the club. I sensed their alarm, but unlike the clubbers, they weren't exactly fleeing in terror. One witch even dared to cross my path—an ice blonde with eyes as dark as coals. A speck of her magic barely rose to the tip of her white staff before I yanked it from her grip and launched it into the street.

"*Don't*," I told her stiffly.

And she didn't. Her dark eyes narrowed at the staff as it fell against the asphalt.

Did I intentionally mean to flex my supernatural muscles?

Hell, yeah.

As much as I didn't want trouble, no one had the right to threaten me or my family in our home. *No one.*

The head witch's back stiffened. She must have felt the swarm of magic leave her lesser's staff. She ignored Taran to fix her eyes on me. And holy cow, the coven must have had a "homely girls need not apply" clause. The witch resembled a blond version of Betty Boop . . . if Betty came chock full of bad attitude.

The amethyst toe rings glimmered with enough power to darken the light blue floorboards, and the heat they emanated was hot enough to burn. No wonder she didn't wear shoes. Girlfriend would scorch right through them. Hate found its way into her lovely brown eyes. "Were you the one who destroyed my sister's talisman?"

"Yup," I said before Taran could answer. I took my place next to Emme. "Now tell me what you're doing here."

And because the situation didn't border on sucky enough, Mrs. Mancuso came to the witch's rescue. She stomped out of her house dressed to the nines in one of her floral housedresses, orthopedic sandals, and her best support hose. "Taran Wird. Leave the Jehovah's Witnesses alone!"

Oh, dear Lord.

"Shut up and die, you old hag!" Taran hissed back.

Mrs. Mancuso pointed a nasty finger—at *me*. "Celia Wird. Do something to control that strumpet sister of yours!"

Strumpet. Now, there's a word you don't hear every day.

I heaved a heavy sigh. "Taran. Please be nice to the Jehovah's Witnesses."

The soft chuckle from the witch near our car caught me by surprise.

"Something funny, Sister Genevieve?" The head witch's voice held a twinge of annoyance, but the magic that danced along her hourglass form demanded an apology. My senses shot to high alert. I didn't like the way they regarded each other. Witches were a lot like Jersey girls. You didn't want to get in between two fighting. Fists, foul mouths, and fake hair would fly.

Genevieve took a small, elegant step away from our Subaru, keeping her magic whoop-ass stick close to her side. "Of course not, Sister Larissa." Her voice was soft and silky, her words nonthreatening and apologetic. Yet she left me thinking she actually meant, "Any time, any place, *bitch*."

The witches, it seemed, weren't as united as I thought. Still, I didn't want them rumbling on our home turf. "Taran, get rid of Mrs. Mancuso," I muttered.

A translucent stream of blue and white smoke swirled from Taran's core. The witches slammed their protective shields around themselves with such force, the magnitude of their power scratched like a wire brush against my skin. They watched, fascinated by Taran's blue and white stream. It glided like a graceful butterfly to where Mrs. Mancuso jabbered on about what tramps we were, and how we'd besmirched a once lovely neighborhood with our hussy ways.

"Go in the house, Mancuso," Taran whispered in an eerie voice. "Your chin hairs need plucking."

Mrs. Mancuso inhaled Taran's magic. Her eyes closed briefly, then with quick determined steps she returned to her house in a trance. "Heathens," she snapped before slamming her red door shut.

Larissa narrowed her eyes at my nose. She was smart enough not to directly challenge my tigress. "What do you want?" I repeated once more.

Larissa rose to her full height. "Your sister's not a witch."

I frowned. "No, she's not."

Larissa pursed her lips. "Yet she wields magic."

No, just fire, lightning, and the occasional mind influence. I didn't care to share that with Larissa and her gal pals, though. "Yes, she has great power."

Larissa honed in on Taran. "How do you do it? How do you work your enchantments?"

Taran stormed forward, her platform pumps clicking against the wooden floorboards. Larissa stood a good six inches taller than my petite sister, but you wouldn't know it by the way Taran faced off with her. "If you must know, I take the magic from the world around me and manipulate it to do what I want."

A few of the coven muffled back gasps while Larissa gaped at Taran like she pimp-slapped her. I didn't understand the issue until Larissa's blanched skin reddened and she wigged out on Taran. "How *dare* you rob the earth of her magic!"

Huh?

Taran exchanged glances with me before scowling back defensively. "I didn't *rob* anything. The magic doesn't stay with me. I give it back the moment I'm done."

A couple of witches scoffed with disgust. There were hushed whispers of "sin" and "blasphemy." Their sanctimonious attitudes pissed. Me. Off. My tigress clawed on the inside, restless to defend Taran. I held her back. If she unleashed, blood would stain the streets. There was no need for blood. Yet.

"You disgrace our sister, and now you mock and spit on our faith." Larissa motioned to the witch with the scroll. "Add the *mortem provocatio.*"

"No." The dark-haired Genevieve's voice was quiet but absolute.

"This isn't your decision, Genevieve," Larissa hissed back. "Add. *It,*" she repeated once more.

Larissa snapped her fingers. Four witches, all armed with staffs, stepped forward. They exchanged hesitant glances, but positioned themselves so that each one of them faced one of us. The spiky-haired witch stumbled her way in between them and handed Emme the scroll she'd prepared. Emme quickly skimmed it, her eyes widening with every passage. "It's a decree challenging each of us to a fight to the death—"

I yanked the scroll from Emme's hands and tore it in half before she could finish reading it. "I invoke the Ninth Law."

Silence fell. The breeze stopped as if switched off, the mourning doves ceased their song, and day abruptly became night. Creepy as hell, yes. But I wasn't going to let a darkening sky distract me from protecting my sisters.

Larissa smiled like one of those hyenas who'd caught a whiff of their prey. "You're the head of the family?" I nodded. Larissa's malicious grin widened. "Then you realize that means you get to face me?"

My tigress eyes replaced my own. "I know what it means." I rammed the pieces of parchment into her chest, shaking with the need to *change*. Larissa clutched the torn scroll against her as she fell, my strike hard enough to make her topple down the steps. I hadn't meant to shove her so hard; in fact, I'd fought to stay in control. Yet little remained to hold back my beast. She didn't like being prey. And neither did I.

Anyone else would have fallen and cracked her head open. There. Challenge over. But Larissa wasn't just anyone. The amethysts on her toes lit the darkness with a ghostly light as an invisible force caught her and lifted her upright. She returned to her place at the edge of my porch, smiling her nasty smile like my hands had never touched her. She opened her arms and let the remains of the parchment fall as she faced me once more. This time, she didn't avert her gaze. "What are your terms?" she asked, her tone casual.

"*Celia.*" I was the tigress, but it was Taran who growled. "What the hell are you doing?"

"Shut up, Taran." Something in my voice made Taran heed my order. Emme and Shayna grabbed each of her hands, keeping her in place, and preventing her from using her magic. I took a breath, trying not to let my tigress unleash. She'd taken Larissa's disrespect as permission to kill. But I needed to fix this mess, not make matters worse. My husky voice dropped an octave. "To be left in peace. If I win, we get to stay and you and your coven are to leave us alone."

Larissa laughed. "And if you win, my coven and I leave Tahoe."

"The Ninth Law doesn't require a death." Genevieve's statement appeared more directed as a reminder to Larissa than as an explanation to my sisters.

Larissa nodded with mock agreement. "No. But should death accidentally befall her . . ." She glanced at me over her shoulder as she sashayed down the wooden steps. "Are we in agreement, my dear?"

My spine stiffened. I followed her to our front walk with my sisters flanking my sides. I barely managed to keep from pouncing on Larissa right then and there. High school had arrived at our front door and the Mean Girls made it clear they didn't like us. And this time they'd put it in writing. "Yes, we're in agreement."

"Very well. Three days. Three challenges." Larissa gave me the once-over as a rush of magic fanned out her skirt. Something about her stare made me think she was taking in more than my outer appearance. "Beast," she stated. "Self," she said meeting my eyes. "Protection," she added with a grin.

"Beast. Self. Protection," the coven chanted.

There was a long, dramatic pause as we waited for an explanation, or at the very least some Cliff Notes. Genevieve scanned the members of her coven. She'd chanted along with her sisters, but she didn't seem happy about it. "You ask a great deal of your clan," she said simply.

Larissa whipped her head to face her. "You speak out of line, Sister Genevieve."

"I don't believe I do, Larissa."

I didn't know much about witch etiquette. But I did know they were supposed to address each other as "sister" or by title, especially in public. Larissa and Genevieve's magic hadn't clashed, but I could sense it brewing to the surface. It would soon boil over into a bloody, messy brouhaha, a brouhaha I had no desire to be a part of. Just because Genevieve didn't appear to like Larissa it didn't mean she was on our side.

Without bothering to glance away, the dark-haired Genevieve spoke again. "Everyone, return to your vehicles. It's time to depart."

Car doors slammed shut and engines roared to life.

One by one, the Jettas sped away.

Only the two head witches remained. Larissa smiled at the other witch with all the pleasantness of a great white shark in the company of a baby seal. "The day will soon come when you, too, shall challenge me. Just like Celia, you will lose, Genevieve."

"The day will come." Genevieve's voice remained soft and silky. "And I will not lose."

Larissa laughed, turning in circles like Julie Andrews on top of a freaking mountain.

Before she disappeared in a crash of thunder that propelled us onto our snow-ridden lawn.

I quickly rolled off of poor Emme and crouched to attack as the rear side window of our sedan snapped and crackled. A chink spread from one end to the other. It continued onto the passenger side window, spelling out words in an ear-splitting pitch like a saw cutting through metal.

Three days.

My sisters and I staggered to our feet, stunned and more shaken than I cared to admit. Larissa didn't *have* to blow out our eardrums, wreck our car, and go all Linda Blair on us. But I supposed when eye of newt and toe of frog-fight fests were concerned, it paid to be over the top.

Genevieve dusted off the snow from her dress and rose on wobbly legs, using her staff for support. She staggered to our driveway, paying no mind to the chunks of charred sidewalk littering the street, or the pizza-sized crevice where Larissa had stood. Her lovely eyes fell upon me before nodding gracefully. "May strength, will, and courage carry you through your task."

We watched with opened mouths as Genevieve spun gracefully, erasing the darkness of night with her gentle breeze.

"*Damn*," Taran said.

Chapter Five

Beast. Self. Protection. We had no clue what that meant exactly. We played around with the words, even did some Googling, trying to prepare for anything and everything. Three days. What did *that* mean? Would each challenge last three days or would they start in three days' time? I wished I'd asked more questions, exchanged digits, requested a rulebook—*something*. But I hadn't. The little we knew about supernaturals wasn't enough, and now it was too late.

Danny appeared stunned stupid when I'd phoned him following the witches' disappearing act. He didn't speak for a solid minute. "Move, Celia," he'd finally insisted. "For the love of all things holy, just *move*. You can come stay with me in Palo Alto." I heard him rifling through papers. "I've done a little research on the Tahoe Clan. This time of year they practice making it rain in Meek's Bay. They sometimes hole up for days chanting. If the majority of the clan is distracted, maybe it will give you and your sisters the chance to escape."

"No matter where we go, there'll just be another Larissa telling us we don't belong. We'll always be different, Danny. There's nothing we can do about that. But that doesn't make it okay for anyone to push us around or force us from our home."

The silence that had followed told me he agreed. But his tone when he'd spoke also echoed his fear. "Celia, I don't want you to die."

"I don't either, Danny," I'd told him truthfully.

We put a hold on our renovations, unsure whether the attacks would arrive on our doorstep or if I'd be summoned to the middle of some cornfield somewhere at the next full moon. My sisters guarded our home in shifts. I focused on getting into optimal shape, exercising, weight training, and making the heavy bag in our half-finished basement my bitch. A week of worrying. A week of waking at every creek, squeak, and crack. And nothing. Finally, we returned to our jobs at the hospital, figuring Larissa wouldn't dare pick a fight in such a public place.

Ha. Ha. Silly me.

I was finishing the last few details of my delivery so I could move on to my next assignment. I smiled at the sleeping infant as I cuddled her in my arms. Our foster mother had been a nurse. It was a career that had never interested me, but one she forced me into when she was diagnosed with cancer. I was only in high school at the time. Ana Lisa made me get my GED, and dragged me kicking and screaming into the program. I resented her for it. But I resented her cancer more. She knew she was dying and wanted me to obtain a job that would secure my future and provide for my siblings. I never expected to love it. But I did. So much so, my sisters pursued nursing as well. Taran worked in the Cardiac Lab. Emme in Hospice. Shayna and I delivered babies—a job that showed us the miracle of life on a daily basis.

My smile widened as I walked toward the new father. The labor and delivery had gone smoothly except the young dad remained skittish. He kept his hands on his lap when I tried to pass him his baby girl.

"I don't think I should hold her," he said.

I rocked the baby when she stirred. Like Tahoe, babies settled my beast and made me less scary. "I think you should. You've been waiting nine months to meet her, haven't you?"

He glanced at his wife, the baby, and me. "What if I break her?"

"You won't."

"What if I drop her?"

"I won't let you."

"What if she dates?"

I pulled out his arm and tucked the sweet infant into the crook. "I think you have a good fifteen years to worry about that one." I reached to help him wrap his other arm around his daughter, but he beat me to the punch. And just like that, the frightened man became a "Daddy." He lifted his chin as the first tears of fatherhood dripped down his face. "Thank you, Celia," he whispered.

I nodded and turned to adjust the new mommy's pillows. Compliments weren't something I was used to, no matter how subtle. I covered the beaming woman with a warm blanket I'd brought from the linen room. "Everything looks great. I'll give you some alone time and be back with your lunch."

The woman squeezed my hand, but never turned away from her precious little family. I slipped quietly out the door with the cartful of garbage from the delivery. I pushed the squeaky wheels along the halls, nodding to a doctor as she passed. As much as the babies brought me great joy, every delivery made me wonder if I'd ever experience that moment myself. I abandoned those thoughts. Who would want to father the child of a beast?

I knocked my elbow against the push knob to open the door to the dirty utility room. The giant metal cage to my right was filled to the brink with bean bags and yoga balls yet to be cleaned. Directly in front of me stood a large sink and the counter where we placed the cord blood for lab pickup. I slapped on some gloves and dumped the placenta into the medical waste bin, and angled the cart next to the laundry and garbage chutes. With speed worthy of any tigress, I dumped the soiled linens down the rusted metal chute, slammed it closed, and opened the one for waste. Everything ran smoothly until a giant tongue sprung from the chute and fastened itself around my waist.

Shit!

My face smacked hard against the brick wall as it pulled, stunning my beast and slowing my reaction time. All I knew was I couldn't go down the bin. My arms and legs spread out to cling to the opening, encouraging the force to yank harder. I grunted, gripping the edge tighter with one hand while my free claws sliced at the tongue holding me.

Warm fluid splashed against my scrubs. I'd thought I'd injured it, but realized quickly I'd only pissed it off. The tongue tightened, robbing me of my breath and threatening to snap my spine. It pulled me, harder and harder, until I wheezed and my body was abruptly yanked through.

I fell down the passage, banging against the metal sides as my claws searched wildly for something to dig into. My claws raked against the metal like a fork, but still I found nothing to halt my descent. The burning in my lungs caused fear to rip through my veins. I reached into my beast, willing her to beat back my panic. We had to survive. No way would we die without a fight.

The opening was too narrow for my beast form to fit through, but even if she could, the strong grip would likely prevent my *change*. So I kicked out, using my legs to prolong my inevitable meet-and-greet with whatever had lassoed me. Every time I slowed, the force became more insistent and my need for air grew ever desperate.

Finally, I managed to stop at the curve in the chute. Only to have something collide with my head and burst open.

Double shit.

I whipped down faster like a reverse bungee. It's bad enough I had a tongue dragging me down a dark cylinder caked with years of hospital nastiness. Now I had to deal with a rainfall of garbage. Mounds of trash pounded into me in a cascade of rubber gloves, plastic cups, and catheters. Globs of iodine, detergents, and things better left wrapped up tight spilled against my head and arms like rain.

The tongue, thankfully, didn't seem to like the combo, either. It quivered as if gagging and loosened its hold. I slashed hard in the direction of the pull just as I hurtled through the basement opening.

My body hit a large container and toppled it over. I rolled from the force and slammed into the cinderblock wall. I moaned and chanted the F-word like it possessed the power to make me rise. It didn't work. I slumped onto my side. Everything hurt down to my toenails.

The expanse of the dingy white room took up an entire hospital wing. I gasped, pushing myself up on all fours in time to hear a wet hiss.

So much for thinking the hospital was neutral territory.

I turned my head, scanning the area. Four bins at each corner, including the one I knocked down. A double door to the far left. A floor buffer. A few broken office chairs. And a newt the size of our sedan hanging upside down from the ceiling. He blinked his tire-sized brown eyes at me, and angled his head. He seemed deep in thought while slurping on the blood pooling in his mouth. Witches, it seemed, didn't mind falling under the "eye of newt" stereotype.

My mind searched for what I knew of California newts. Brown, smooth skins. Check. Orange bellies. Check. Long tongue. Not sure, but I gave that one a check.

Hundreds of times more poisonous than cyanide if ingested? Oh, yeah.

Witches. Didn't. Play. Fair.

Beast against beast, but at a cost. If I bit into him with my fangs I'd die within minutes. But that didn't mean I couldn't claw, couldn't strike, couldn't kick. I slowly rose to my feet. The muscles and girth of my golden tigress stretched the thin cotton fabric of my scrubs until blue shredded scraps plopped against my fuzzy paws. It was a show of intimidation and to catch my breath. *Take that, Geico reject.*

The newt angled his head from side to side, curious yet not afraid. Oh, so not afraid. His limbs extended outward, his eyes depressed, and his tail whipped eagerly. He wanted to brawl. But so did my beast.

He leapt from the ceiling, slamming his head through the concrete wall when I jumped. But either he had eyes in the back of his head or Larissa saw all. His tail whipped me across the face. Warm fluid drenched my eye and sudden pain stung beneath my fur like fire. My head flew back. I slammed into the group of broken office chairs, cracking them with the weight of my form. I scrambled to my feet and charged. He jerked free and rammed me into one of the bins. I *shifted*, came up behind him as human and kicked him in the jaw when he spun to face me.

His skull snapped back, but the bones of his neck didn't break. I straddled his head and used my weight and muscle to flip him onto his side, ramming my clawed hands into his brown eyes. The mutilated tongue rushed out and nailed me in the face like a fist. I fell back and *shifted*, sparing my body from the brunt of the fall.

My molecules traveled beneath the foundation and reformed as I surfaced behind him. He must have sensed my presence. His tail whipped across my shins before I could strike. I collided face first into the concrete. The impact robbed my lungs of much needed air. The newt leapt on me, slapping at me with his leathery hands and ramming me in the back of the head with his bloody tongue.

I saw stars. And planets. And rockets. And possibly Superman. But he wasn't there to save me, and I'd be damned if I'd let Larissa win.

Without enough breath, I couldn't *shift*. But I could *change*. My tigress form returned. I rolled, clawing and cleaving into the soft underbelly of the newt. His skin parted like wet cardboard. I wrenched my head to the side, trying to avoid the likely poisonous blood and entrails drenching my fur. He screeched, ruptured eyes oozing fluid as he whipped the remains of his tongue to encircle my throat.

I raked his tongue with my free paw before he could squeeze. A section of it fell with a splat beside me as I dug my front and back legs into the large holes of his underside. Adrenaline fueled my strength, numbing me to the sweltering pain. I launched him into the corner garbage bin. He landed hard enough to pop the overstuffed bags, spilling dirty cups and pizza boxes onto the linoleum.

I whirled onto my belly and roared. *Get up! Get up!* Dammit, I was *pissed*.

My tigress didn't like getting thrown around. And my human side didn't care for it, either. For a long time, the newt didn't move. But the moment his dark brown tail lifted, I bolted and hurdled myself on top of him. My claws hacked into his reptilian side like nails through plastic—hard at first, until I completely broke through the tough outer flesh. His skin and innards sprayed my face in chunks, his squeals barely audible over my thunderous roars.

I continued to slash until I felt the pull of muscle and ligaments from long thin bones. That's when I stopped. Viciousness had its limits, and I'd far surpassed them. I leapt from the bin with grace, the soaked pads of my paws leaving prints on the grimy floor with each step.

I'd won the first challenge. No one appeared with a medal to place around my fuzzy neck, no balloons dropped down from the ceiling, no one patted my back to say, "Well done!" And while I didn't exactly expect a supernatural parade complete with black cats on unicycles, I had expected something more . . . *mystical.* I *changed,* returning to my human side and adding bloody human footprints to the tiger ones. *Now what?* I stood naked again, with no bouncer in a tacky T-shirt in sight. I reached the floor polisher and sighed, exhausted and still freaked out.

If it wasn't for the sudden change in the air, I wouldn't have sensed the giant newt springing at me. With more reflex than strategy, I gripped the handlebars of the floor polisher and swung. The newt bounced off the wall and slumped in front of me, nothing more but ground, battered meat and bone piercing through rubberlike skin.

This time, I needed to make sure he was dead. I bashed in his skull until my face dripped with red death and I couldn't see, only feel. Feel the bones crunch like wet marbles, feel the warm blood turn cold against my heated flesh, feel my muscles scream with stress and tension.

"Miss Celia, what are you do-eeng?"

I jumped and dropped the handlebars. My hands slapped at my saturated face, trying to see through the glop. Eduardo, one of the day-shift custodians, stood by the double doors with a mini version of the trash bins on wheels. I gaped at my bloody hands, then at the blood pooling from my chin onto the floor. My eyes searched the confines of the room. No other blood but mine in sight. The cracked cinderblock had repaired itself, the pizza boxes, cups, and other garbage had returned to the heap. And the broken chairs lay piled neatly in the corner. Absolutely no other evidence of a high-noon magical showdown . . . with the exception of a very small, very dead, very mutilated newt the size of my palm near my feet. This was more the ending to round one I'd expected, minus Eduardo.

"Um. Hi, Eduardo." I pointed to the newt. "I was killing that lizard thingy," I responded with total sincerity.

Eduardo didn't bother to take in the newt. Just me. Go figure. "But why are you bleed-eeng . . . and nay-ked?"

My hands gripped my girl parts. *Oh, God.*

I ripped one of the giant red medical waste bags off a hook and wrapped it around me like a towel. "It's a long story." Well. Not really. "Can I borrow your phone, Eduardo?" My face matched the color of the bag perfectly. Good heavens, how many more men could see me naked?

Eduardo's head jerked from the phone at his hip, right back to me. He shook his head, quite hysterically I might add. "No. No. Dees ees no good, Miss Celia. Dees is berry, berry bad." Eduardo abandoned his bin and backed away like I carried a grenade and had asked him if he wouldn't mind holding the pin.

"Eduardo, wait—"

He didn't. And for the second time in a week, I found myself on top of a male, naked. Eduardo was pretty damn slippery for a human, or maybe my sweat-soaked and bloody skin had something to do with it. I held him down while I phoned Shayna. I guessed she called Emme and someone reached out to Taran. They skidded into the bowels of the hospital within minutes to find me dripping with newt juice, naked, and riding a custodian like Sea Biscuit.

Taran took my reptilian romp, well, just as I'd expected.

"Son of *bitch*. You wrestled a lizard!"

"Newt," I muttered while Emme healed me. The gash across my face was wide open. No wonder Eduardo kept screaming. Or perhaps he had a fear of newts.

Shayna borrowed the mop Eduardo carried in his bin to wash clean the footprints. "I don't like this, dude.

You could have been killed. And this was only round one."

"But I wasn't."

Taran's breath increased like she'd run a marathon. "That stupid bitch." Tears streaked down her face. "You should have let me handle this, Celia. If you'd hadn't invoked that God damned Ninth Law—"

"Then we would all be fighting for our lives," I finished for her. My skin tightened as Emme's pale yellow light fused my flesh to seal my wounds. With her power, there wouldn't even be a scar. That didn't mean healing didn't hurt like a mofo. I gritted my teeth as the burning sensation receded. "I think they came to slap us around, with the hopes that maybe they could find an excuse to kill us. But you using magic from the earth was their excuse to issue a death challenge." I squeezed her hand. "We've discussed this, Taran. This is the only way to get what we want."

Taran scowled. "What if you don't make it? The newt's poisoned skin is proof she wouldn't lose sleep if you died."

Shayna swept up the remains of my rival and tossed the little critter in a small trash can. Her thin brows frowned with worry and fear. A single tear fell, streaking a line down her pixie face.

Emme kept her head down. Her timid soul allowed her tears to fall in tandem, never one to hold back her emotions, but always slightly embarrassed she couldn't bury them as deeply as I could. I envied her in a way. I wished I could cry then, or scream from the wickedness of it all. But I couldn't. I never could. I recognized my sisters were no longer the frightened children I had once shielded. They were grown, independent women, capable of living on their own and surviving. Yet despite their self-rule and strength, they still fed from my courage. So I didn't weep, didn't scream, didn't tear the room apart. Even though I very much wanted to.

I placed my hand on her shoulder. "Look. If it comes down to me dying, I'll plead *misericordia*, I promise."

Emme's soft green eyes glistened. "Wh-what if she doesn't honor your surrender?"

I didn't know how to answer her. Lying fell under my Things I Didn't Do list. "Well, let's just hope that she does." My words did little to comfort my sisters and disturbed Eduardo even more. He wriggled beneath me frantically. I hauled him to his feet and held him in front of Taran as Emme's light receded. "Make sure he forgets everything he saw." I glimpsed at my naked and blood-caked form. "*Everything.*"

Chapter Six

Another night passed without me sleeping. Dueling with witches was for the birds—birds who apparently didn't require an ounce of shut-eye. Exhausted as my tigress claimed we felt, I welcomed the day when the rising sun peeked beneath my shades. "Let's get this over with, Larissa," I muttered and stumbled out of bed.

I padded along the dark hardwood floors into the half-tiled bathroom in a tank top and panties—my dress of choice for bed. The architect had designed two master suites. Taran had the other one. Emme and Shayna seemed excited just to have their own rooms for once. I adjusted the spaghetti strap that had fallen from my shoulder after I finished washing my face. I reached for my toothbrush and got down to business. Crap, my mouth seemed so dry.

My reflection showed me I looked just as bad as I felt. Dark circles swirled around my green eyes, the muscles of my shoulders and arms strained with tension, and my big hair had reached Monsters of Rock proportions. If men hadn't found me scary before, they sure as hell would now.

I rinsed my mouth and reached for my towel. I

wiped my lips, frowning when my white towel somehow appeared pink in the mirror. My eyes scanned the bathroom, searching for something that might be affecting the color. I turned back and jumped when my reflection greeted me with a smile that wasn't mine and two big middle fingers. *Omigod.* My mirror image threw back her head and laughed. I didn't. I also didn't blow myself a kiss.

My knees buckled under me and I staggered back, slamming into the double doors as I watched my reflection leap over the tiled counter and land in a crouch on the floor. She rose slowly, her messy hair falling around her face and shoulders, watching me with hungry and sinister eyes. Her tongue slid across her upper lip. She tasted my fear.

And she liked it.

To fuel my terror she turned her head to the side and kept going. The crunching and snapping of her neck made me cringe. Echoes of her laughter filled the suite until the back of her long tresses hung over her breasts—my breasts. Oh, *God.* Her head whipped back and she smiled with glee, pleased by my horror.

Self. I had to fight my . . . *self.*

I continued to gape until her shoulders collided into my stomach and jetted me into my bedroom. The back of my skull became one with the footboard of my sleigh bed. And that's when my tigress snapped to. I dug my fingers into her hair and wrenched it back. It felt just . . . like . . . my . . . hair—further wigging me out. She screamed with my voice as I wrenched her off me. We rolled on the floor punching and clawing each other. Her blows and scratches were as hard as mine, but mine were more strategic. I raked my claws across her chest, missing her throat by less than an inch. Her eyes widened with fear. She knew I was going to kill her. She knew she needed reinforcements. And she knew where to find them.

Frantic pounding and yelling ensued outside my door. "Celia? Dude, are you okay?" Shayna wiggled the knob. "It's locked."

That's when Bad Celia got dirty. "Help me! Shayna, please help me!"

"Move!" Shayna yelled. A machete cut through the crease in the door and yanked to the side. With a grunt, Shayna splintered the door open.

"Holy *shit*!" Taran screamed when she found me kicking my own ass.

Larissa's other-me and I rolled into Emme, knocking her into Shayna. She screamed. "Which one is Celia?"

"Celia!" Taran yelled. "Tell us something only you would know."

"Like what?" the other me asked in my same raspy voice.

Screw that. I nailed her in the mouth so she couldn't speak, which earned me a jolt of lightning from Taran. My teeth chattered and my hair smoked. "That's her!" Taran yelled, motioning toward me.

"Dude! Are you sure?" Shayna asked, her machete pointed dangerously in my direction.

"Of course I am! That bitch is trying to keep her from telling us the stuff only Celia knows."

I kicked Bad Celia off me and launched a discarded screwdriver into her stomach. Unfortunately, her speed mimicked mine. She dove out of the way and into the bathroom. It would have nailed Emme had she not blocked it with her *force*. The screwdriver fell with a loud clang. Emme glanced from it to me, appearing crushed I could do such a thing, further reinforcing that I was the imposter.

Taran scowled hard enough to burn. Her irises went white as she gathered the full gamut of her power while the other Celia draped against the doorframe pretending to be hurt. She winked at me once just as Taran screamed, "*Get her!*"

I skidded back on my butt, just missing the machete

Shayna pitched between my legs. My eyes crossed as I watched it bat back and forth in front of my nose. Never had I been more grateful to be female.

I swallowed hard, but didn't hesitate. Every hair on my body stuck out from the energy Taran built into her lightning. I flung my body through my bedroom window. Glass scraped across my fur like red hot tuning forks. I landed on four paws as a giant bolt of blue and white exploded onto the lawn. The force of the blast threw me along the deep snow face-first. I bolted to the greenbelt behind our house, half-blind, barely out of reach of the next strike.

My paws dug into the thick snow, kicking it up behind me as I raced up the hill. I ground to a halt about a half mile away. I needed to get far enough away to form a plan, but not so far that I'd leave my sisters alone with Larissa's creation. They trusted her, and while the challenge was only supposed to include me, their trust could end up placing them in danger.

My claws scratched at the ground restlessly. It killed me to leave them, but if I stayed I'd have to fight them. All of them. Someone would get hurt. And I'd rather die than hurt my family.

I crouched behind a tree, my fur already saturated from the snow. But it beat *changing* to stand naked once more. I growled, cursing Larissa, her mother, and her damn pets if she owned any. The freak probably kept a rabid canary for kicks and giggles.

Okay. Now what?

Thunder roared above me. A thick black cloud inched its way across the sky until it covered the weak winter sun, dropping the temperature about ten more degrees. Sleet mixed with snow, and wind almost immediately followed. Okay. This didn't suck or anything. Larissa's power likely also included manipulating the weather. Icy rain pierced my skin like nails and a gust of wind slapped a mound of snow into my face.

Bitch.

I panted hard, both with fear and anger. Larissa played a cruel game, but to turn my sisters against me told me she also played damn smart. I supposed it was too much to hope a Walmart greeter could have been crowned head witch. Now, there was a friendly soul.

I waited and waited and waited some more. My tigress ears strained to hear any screams or cries over the howling wind and falling sleet. After about an hour of waiting, I made my way down to the house, keeping low and close to the thick brush surrounding the perimeter of our property. Everything seemed quiet. Too quiet. The lights were on in the kitchen and in the large open family room. The first level sat higher above ground. I couldn't see over the deck railing.

I searched around for the fir with the thickest trunk and climbed. FYI, tigers weren't meant to scale evergreens. My big body swayed back and forth like a set of windshield wipers. Pine needles found their way up my nose. Icicles pelted me in the head, and branches slapped more snow in my face. Finally, I climbed enough to see . . . my sisters and the evil Celia gathered around the fireplace sipping steaming mugs of tea and playing Yahtzee.

I just about fell out the tree. What the hell? Whose side were they on, anyway?

I scrambled down with all the grace of a rhino, landing hard on my wet rump. Enough was enough. Bad Celia was going down. Insult knew no injury like this. My paws dug into the snow, crunching through the icy surface and into the soft white stuff I now officially hated. My eyes focused on the warm glow of the family room lights as I crept, my claws itching to cut. No longer could I see them, but I could sense them. I needed to get my double away from my family and outside to me.

My roar signaled my arrival, long, strong, clear.

Shayna bolted onto the deck first. Her movements so quick, I thought she merely pointed in my direction. The tip of her knife sliced into my tail. I hissed. My tigress had barely rolled us out of the way before Shayna could strike a vital organ. I roared again, challenging Larissa's Celia to come down. She inched her way to the edge of the deck and narrowed her eyes.

Crap. I guess I was pretty damn scary. My sisters backed away from her all at once. Shayna lifted another dagger, and Taran's hands fired with white and blue. Bad Celia glanced back at them, appearing genuinely confused. "What?" she asked.

Emme clasped her hand over her mouth. "Y-you're not our Celia."

"Of course, I am," she said.

Taran's jaw clenched tight. "Then why aren't you *changing* and going after her? Why are you letting Shayna fight her for you?"

Yeah! They figured it out, knowing I'd never permit them to fight my battles. Now we had her. *Watcha gonna do now, poser?*

The other Celia shrugged. Then *changed* into a golden tigress and leapt off the deck.

Shit to the seventh power.

Like my human likeness, the golden tigress resembled mine to perfection. Larissa's power should have shocked me stupid. Instead all it did was rile my beast. I remained a very still, very pissed-off statue for roughly two-point-five seconds. My rage slapped my astonishment upside the head like I was a spoiled heiress. I charged my other half and rammed into her with my claws out. There remained only one true me. And my beast planned to keep it that way.

We fell into a tumble of furious fangs and wicked claws. Her incisors dug into my shoulder. I pushed back the stabbing pain and surrendered to my beast. Larissa's creation didn't possess the thick hide of my tigress, nor did she hold that animalistic intuition and viciousness to survive. I shredded through the loose fur and into the tender muscle beneath until the snow streaked with crimson and chunks of fur. My victim roared in agony, the sounds mimicking my tigress's voice so closely, it became almost too much to bear. So I focused on my task rather than the virtual hamburger Larissa attempted to make of my brain. My sisters screamed, likely unsure whether the real Celia suffered or not, and torn whether to act.

As my fangs found the imposter's jugular, she *changed* back, resuming her human form. My sisters gathered around, their power accelerating from their distress, but failing to act. Their gazes danced from me to her when I dropped her on the ground. They seemed unsure who to attack, who to defend.

"*Fuck,*" Taran sobbed.

My stomach lurched when I saw what they saw—my small body reduced to nothing more than frayed chunks of flesh. Ribs shone white and slick, protruding with each torturous breath. Hair stuck to the deep gashes on my face—her face. *Sweet Jesus. What's happening?* My eyes burned and my head spun, no longer able to distinguish the illusion from a very twisted reality.

The imposter reached a hand toward Emme, blood spurting out of her mouth as she spoke. "Help me, Emme. Please help me."

Emme extended her hands, her palms glowing with that soft pale light, ready to heal, ready to mend, ready to save. Just before their fingertips touched, Emme stumbled backward, falling on her backside. Tears streamed down her face. She shook her head and covered her ears, wrestling with her contradictory emotions.

Shayna dropped her blade. It fell flat against the layer of ice beside her. Her face blanched and her hands shook as she tried to find her words. "Is she . . . Could she . . ."

I couldn't take the suffering. I *changed*, falling into a kneeling position to cradle the other Celia's naked body against me. She felt cold—my God, so *cold*—her skin supple and moist against mine. I pushed her red-stained curls from her face. She appeared so innocent then, young, helpless, incapable of harming another soul, the menace of her beast nowhere in sight.

She locked her gaze on mine just before I snapped her neck.

The crunch of her vertebrae made me drop to my side. Shayna and Emme choked back screams. Taran hollered with rage and grief, dropping to her knees next to me with her flaming blue and white hands inches from my face. The heat roasted my skin. I recoiled as if burned, unable to take the breadth of her fire. Something in my expression made her stop mere seconds before setting me aflame. Perhaps it was my own horror staring back at her, or maybe the fact that I didn't fight back. Either way she stopped. Thank heaven she stopped.

I bit my bottom lip hard enough to taste blood, unable to take the tormented grimace wrinkling Taran's beautiful face. So instead I focused on the burden I still held in my arms, and how the slight weight suddenly seemed unbearable. Her lifeless green eyes continued to stare at my face, despite her lolling head. I wanted to toss her away, deep into the pine forest. It wasn't really me after all, was it? But I couldn't seem to do that to myself. So I sat there, watching, waiting, while my sisters' cries reverberated against my skull.

The thick clouds above vanished like a vial of ink poured into the ocean. The strong wind and freezing sleet ceased. Slowly, Larissa's creation dissolved into water, clean and pure, creating tiny rivers against the blood-stained snow. When she finally disappeared, all that remained was a small clump of my hair draped against my knee.

I barely felt Taran and Shayna helping me to stand. Shayna said something about hypothermia, but I couldn't be sure, nor did I really care. I swallowed hard. In my arms, I had held the dead me. And nothing would ever wipe that memory.

Chapter Seven

"I want to kill her. Just let me kill her. Damn it, Celia. Will you look at me?"

"I am looking at you, Taran."

The shock of my experience receded as Emme encased me in her healing aura and Shayna threw about seven blankets over my shivering form. Except Emme's gift and Shayna's attention failed to erase the images of the fight. They continued to haunt me, but at least now I could function. Sort of.

Taran paced around the kitchen, balls of blue and white forming, disintegrating, and reforming in her palms. Her agitation and growing hate threatened to burn down our house. I wanted to calm her and reinforce the fact that only one challenge remained. Yet I couldn't even stop my body from shaking. I'd killed myself. And while my rational side insisted that it was just part of Larissa's mindscrew, it remained one hell of an illusion. The other Celia's skin had felt like my skin. Her eyelashes fanned out thick and long like mine, her green eyes sparked just as intensely, just as sharply. Larissa had mimicked my physique to a T, down to the freckle on the knuckle of my right pinky. Witches vowed to do no harm.

I supposed that remained true. So long as you didn't piss one off.

Shayna's back rested against our new granite top, her arms crossed. She no longer cried. No one did. I wished then she would, hoping the release might soothe her. "I could have killed you." Her head angled my way. "I never miss. You know I never miss. This was the first time I didn't hit my mark. If it wasn't for your tigress side I would have . . ." I expected her to burst into tears then, but she only shook her head before turning toward the window.

"Shit." Taran abandoned her fire and leaned into the counter, burying her face into her hands. "We all could have killed you, Celia." Her carefully applied mascara smeared down her cheeks. She clenched her jaw when she regarded me once more. "I'll find that bitch Larissa, Ceel. And when I do, I swear I'll end this."

"And have every last witch in the Tahoe region after us?" I shook my head. "No. You've already seen what one can do. And I think both of us have done our share of killing. Don't you?"

Taran didn't answer. She pursed her lips. In the end, murder was murder, no matter how just. Emme and Shayna had never experienced taking a life. And I hoped they never would. That's one of the reasons I'd pounced on the Ninth Law. I didn't want them to have someone's heart stop by their hands. Taran and I? Hell, some nights I still woke to the screams of those who'd killed our parents. They'd begged me to spare them when I hunted them down. I didn't. Not a one. Most people would have expected a fifteen-year-old to show some mercy. But I suppose most people would have given me too much credit.

I rubbed my face, willing my thoughts to concentrate on the here and now. Fatigue weighed on my muscles like a heavy mound of sand. Emme took almost ten minutes to heal the damage Taran, Shayna, and Larissa had unleashed. A personal record for her, but my injuries had been extensive and now my body griped, exhausted from its efforts to help her. "One challenge left," I managed to mutter. "Tomorrow, at midnight, this should all be behind us."

Shayna raised a brow. "Will you make it till midnight, dude? These challenges aren't getting easier." She played with the edges of her long ponytail. "And God knows we're not helping."

"It all ends tomorrow night," I promised them. And it would. Except I couldn't predict who would stand as the victor. I never expected the challenge to be easy. And yet my naiveté never prepared me for this.

"Celia, I'm not sure what to think of all this," Emme said almost silently.

Which part—the newt, the challenge, or Celia vs. Celia? "What do you mean, sweetie?"

Emme reached for the ice cream in the freezer and pulled the milk from the double door fridge. "I thought witches were like vampires in that they couldn't cross our threshold to do us harm—unless we invited them in, I mean."

I massaged the tense muscles of my left shoulder. "Technically they didn't harm me. I harmed myself. My body—or whatever—did have a right to be here."

Emme smiled softly. "But they needed a bit of your essence to enter. And I presume they managed that through the use of your hair. But how could they obtain such a large clump without entering our house?"

"They took it from the hospital." I elaborated when Shayna stopped fumbling beneath the counter for the blender and frowned with obvious confusion. "I had too much slop on me following the first attack and showered at work. I normally finger-comb my waves after I wash my hair and let them air dry. But all the body fluid had glued my strands together. I borrowed your comb from our locker, Shayna, and worked it through my hair to get everything out. It was pretty much shot when I finished with it, so I tossed it. Larissa could obviously see me. That's how she'd caught me in the dirty utility room. She, or her witches, could have seized my leftover hair from the drain or fished the comb from the garbage." Shayna blinked back at me. "I, um, owe you a new comb," I said in response to her blank expression.

Shayna rushed to her feet and threw her arms around me. "I don't care about the stupid comb," she choked. "I care about you. She could have cast a lot worse spell with your hair and blood in her hands."

"*God damn it.*" Taran scooped the vanilla ice cream into the blender like it had called her a bitch and poured in what remained of the milk. Most of it sloshed off to the sides, spilling all over the brown and black granite counter. I grabbed a towel to wipe it, but she ripped it from my grasp. "For shit's sake, Celia. Shayna's right. Who knows what else Larissa plans to do? With your hair, your blood— Aw, *hell*. Why didn't you throw in a tooth while you were at it?"

"If the newt had managed to pry off a molar, maybe I would have." My dark humor was supposed to make them laugh. Only silence greeted me. Silence, and the still air that came with an ill-fated future. Taran hit the mix button on the blender. She poured me a milkshake the moment the mixer stopped. I downed it and she poured me another, giving me the much needed calories I'd need to fight. Popeye had his spinach. My tigress, well, what can I say. She liked her milk.

Shayna rushed down to the basement and returned with more ice cream and more milk. My appetite surprised even me. When I had my fill, I dumped my empty glass into the dishwasher and headed up the back steps, hoping my tired body would surrender into sleep the moment it hit the bed.

Taran gripped my arm as my bare feet felt the crush of our newly carpeted steps. Her irises sparkled so clearly, they resembled diamonds instead of sapphires. "Just know this, Celia," she said. "If she hurts you beyond repair, if she doesn't stay true to her word, or if she steals you from us, we *will* go after them. All of them. And God help anyone who takes their side.

Chapter Eight

Weres could sniff lies. So could vampires. And even witches sensed a fib to some extent. I didn't have that gift. But I knew my sisters, sometimes better than I knew my own tigress. Taran meant what she said. And it scared the hell out of me. But what scared me more were the definitive nods from Shayna and Emme.

If something happened, they would avenge me, even at the cost of their own lives. I couldn't fault them. I'd do the same. Yet that didn't make it the right or honorable solution. My narrowed eyes made them drop their gazes. "No, you won't. I invoked the Ninth Law to guarantee your safety, not so you'd kamikaze if the outcome didn't suit you."

"Celia—"

"Enough, Taran. I won't hear anymore. You *will* stay out of it."

I stormed up the steps. My sisters' threats angered and saddened me. I fell into my bed wrestling with what could happen if I failed. Would my stubbornness keep me from calling mercy in time? I hoped not, but I couldn't be sure. Eventually though, the stress of the challenges and the toll they'd taken on my body kicked my worries aside and caused my lids to droop. Darkness claimed me. I fought it at first, afraid the ghosts of my past and the mind games Larissa played would trigger my worst nightmares. I didn't expect pleasant dreams. I didn't expect *him* to return.

I didn't know his name. I couldn't see his face. But I knew his arms. They were strong, stronger than mine, enveloping me with protection and an unspoken promise that I wasn't alone. My fingers traced a line along the powerful ridges of his muscular chest.

"Hi," I whispered when he drew me closer.

"Hi, love," he answered in a voice that wasn't really a voice, just a mere shadow of what could be. "I haven't felt you against me in so long."

"I know. I've missed you." My smile faded. "I'm scared," I confessed. Because it was only to him I could openly admit such weakness.

"You've been scared before."

"Yes, more times than I can count." I listened to his heartbeat, taking comfort in the soft, reassuring drum. "The fear, the threats—they don't end, do they? I'm still not safe."

"No." His voice seemed gruff, angry. Like my fear or the possibility of me getting hurt was too much for him to take. Or maybe I just needed him to sound that way.

I rubbed my face against him, purring softly when his fingers ran gently along my unclothed back. With him, I didn't feel the need to cover my body. It was only right for our bare flesh to touch. "Will you be with me tomorrow?"

"I'm always with you, Celia. You just don't know it yet. . . ."

I woke to the wonderful smell of bacon, my arms clutching a pillow tight, my cheek moist from the tears on my sheets. I cried whenever I dreamt of him, mostly because he remained a figment of my wildest dreams. After all, the possibility of a male's loving arms around me was the furthest thing from reality. Males didn't seek my company, period. So how could I ever convince one to hold me, to touch me, to see me as beautiful?

I wiped my eyes and slipped on a pair of yoga pants before making my way into the bathroom. Brushing my teeth would never be the same again. I paused in front of the mirror. It took several long, tension-filled minutes before I became convinced my reflection wouldn't choke the snot out of me. I reached for my toothbrush and some paste, all the while glaring at my potential would-be assassin.

My original plan included making my bed, except the wonderful smell of delicious artery-clogging goodness made me abandon those efforts. I quickly padded down the steps, grateful I'd survived the morning's teeth-cleansing experience.

Shayna's bright smile greeted me in the kitchen. The window spilling the bright morning sun made her blink as she passed. Good grief, I must've slept a hell of a long time.

She gave me a one-arm hug, careful not to spill the batter-filled bowl in her opposite arm. "Hey, dude. I made you your favorite: bacon, bacon, and more bacon."

I frowned, pretending to be annoyed. "No omelets to go with that bacon?"

She slapped her palm against her forehead. "Oh! How could I have been so dense? Don't worry, Ceel. I'm on it."

I grabbed the silverware and plates and started arranging them along the elevated bar. Shayna placed the bowl on the counter and lifted everything from my grasp. "Ah, ah, ah. You have a long day ahead of you. I'll take care of it. Could you go see what's keeping Taran? She promised to help with waffle duty."

"Oh, sure."

Taran's room lay directly below mine on the first floor. She liked having the level to herself. I supposed it allowed the independence she'd always sought, all the while keeping us close. I knocked on her door. "Taran? You awake?" I knocked harder when she didn't answer. "Taran?"

I opened the door, figuring I'd let her sleep if I found her snoozing. My tigress and I could take on waffle duty if necessary. No need to disturb sleeping beauty. And maybe I'd serve her breakfast in bed. God knew we all deserved a bit of kindness.

Taran's frilly white linens lay scattered on the floor next to her four-poster bed. Like me, she had a king-sized bed. But unlike me, she'd soon have someone to keep her warm between the sheets. Lack of company wasn't an issue for Taran. It was more that most males failed to keep her interest for long. The bad boys tended to bore her over time, and the good ones never seemed good enough. Too bad. Deep beneath her tough outer shell and short fuse, Taran's heart radiated enough heat to warm those she loved. I often wondered who would capture her heart—and if he could handle the love she had to give.

I lifted her sheets and tossed them over the navy comforter crumpled into one giant heap. She must have had a rough night of sleep in anticipation of the day. The light shone from the open double-doors to her five-piece bathroom. I stepped in. "Taran?"

The large open bathroom appeared empty, nothing but a stack of cobalt blue and white tiles on the side wall waiting to be mortared in place by our contractor. The freshly tiled countertop remained undisturbed. A row of expensive cosmetics lined the neatly arranged shelf just above the slowly running faucet. *Drip, drip. Drip, drip.*

But still no Taran. No . . . anything.

I shut off the water. Taran only rose early to make our seven a.m. shift start. Shopping remained her preferred choice of exercise, and the stores hadn't yet opened. She didn't take long walks to contemplate the meaning of life. And she knew better than to wander off alone during the Salem Celia Trial. I glanced over my shoulder, hoping against all hope she'd unravel herself from the jumbled mess on the bed.

"Taran?"

My voice cracked as a chill crept its way down my spine like a centipede. "Are you upstairs waking Emme?" I asked for the sake of my sanity. But in reality, I knew she wasn't with Emme. My preternatural hearing didn't pick up any movement on the second floor—nor did it hone in on any voices—just Shayna in the kitchen, whistling as she chopped the ingredients for my omelet.

I inched my way to Taran's walk-in closet, my claws ready to replace my nails. "Shayna!" I called. "Come in here. Something's wrong."

The whistling ceased abruptly as my sweaty palms pushed opened the door of the room-sized closet. My heart stopped when something blocked the door from opening all the way. I didn't force it, choosing to slink through the narrow opening.

I found Taran. Hanging from a noose fashioned from her prized scarves. Her bare feet swayed in a circular motion from where the pieces of silk had been knotted to the railing. A small, overturned vanity chair lay tilted against the boxes of her pricey shoes and the clump of clothes she'd tossed onto the floor to make room for the loop. Her chin slumped against the note pinned to her lacey white nightie. *Mea culpa*, it read—My fault.

I staggered into the mountainous clothes rack behind me, my heart aching from how hard it pummeled my ribcage. Pain gurgled in my throat. I tried to scream. Nothing came out. I willed my trembling body to act. It betrayed me, keeping me cemented to where I stood helplessly trying to scream.

"Taran," I finally squeaked. "Taran . . . *Taran!*"

My legs propelled me forward, jumping onto the railing that held her and bringing the whole damned thing down. More clothes and shoe boxes tumbled over me as my claws sliced through the scarves fastened around her neck. I dragged her back into the bathroom and onto the floor. I jerked when I lay her against the cold foundation. Her sickly green pallor told me she was gone even before my quivering fingertips searched for a pulse that no longer beat.

I screamed for Shayna and Emme as I pounded on our sister's chest. "Wake up, Taran! *Wake up!*" My arms grew weaker and heavier with every thrust. I don't know how long I performed CPR before I realized Shayna wasn't coming. Or Emme.

And that no one answered my calls.

I covered my mouth as I backed away from my dead sister, knocking over the ceramic tiles that scraped against my calves. With legs that stumbled more than walked, and a heart that had no business racing so fast, I lurched my way into the kitchen, where the smell of burning bacon beckoned me forward.

Chapter Nine

The tears welling in my eyes blurred my vision. At first I thought it was better that way. I didn't want to see what awaited me. I didn't want to feel it, either.

But I saw it. And I felt it. And it hurt so much more than I expected.

The knife Shayna used to dice the red peppers and onions into pretty little cubes stuck out from her sternum. Her left leg was bent at a right angle against the bottom of the stove, while the other extended to the opposite cabinet. She twitched as if seizing while bacon grease splattered on her face from the burning pan above. Blood squirted from her mouth as she slanted her head in my direction.

Jesus. She was still alive.

I rushed to her, slipping over the sea of scarlet flowing away from her thin frame. "Oh, God, Shayna!"

I held her body against me, causing the blood beneath her to saturate my hands and thighs as it poured. My sobs rolled out of me in one horrible wretch.

Shayna smiled—*smiled*, her lips and teeth soiled with her lifeline. Her hand slapped my face weakly. I gripped it against my cheek as if it could somehow keep her in this world. She shook her head. And that's when I realized she didn't want me to save her. She was saying good-bye. She knew nothing could help her now.

Except maybe Emme.

I bolted up the steps with Shayna in my arms, falling on my knees more than once on weedy legs. "Emme! *Emme!*"

I kicked opened the door and lay Shayna on Emme's snow-white carpet. As I swayed toward her bed, I already knew what to expect. Yet it didn't stop me from throwing back her dainty pink-and-rose-colored quilt.

Emme's face seemed more angelic in death despite her pale lips, despite her slack mouth, despite her clouded eyes. I shook her limp form hard. "Don't you leave! Your sister needs you. *Your sister needs you!*"

I shook her harder and harder, until my shakes turned into that gentle rocking my mother soothed us with as children. It always comforted Emme. Always. Would it comfort her now? My gulps and wails seemed to come from someone else, too loud, too desperate, too frail to be from me. "Why did you have to die, baby?" I asked as my grief soaked her face. "Don't you know I need you, too?"

The babbling of secretions followed by one long hiss from Shayna's mouth told me she was gone, too. And just like that my heart broke in one, two, three pieces. Symbolizing the loss of the only family I had left.

Numbness masked and eventually dried my sorrow. Slowly I let Emme slide back onto the bed. With the greatest of care, I arranged her perfect blond waves around her sweet face and closed her mouth and eyes. I kissed her forehead, just as I'd done when she was little and missed our mother's touch. I straightened her legs and then positioned Shayna next to her with their hands touching.

They'd want to be together, I thought wearily. I tucked the quilt against their sides, not wanting them to be cold. *Maybe Taran would want to be with them, too,* I reasoned.

I stumbled down the steps, passing by the kitchen phone. I picked up the receiver and punched in some numbers, figuring I should call . . . someone. But the numbers didn't make sense and formed strange symbols I couldn't make out.

"I should do laundry," I decided as an afterthought.

I gathered the dirty towels from every bathroom, confused why I felt so cold and why my hands continued to tremble. I thought I heard someone ask me a question, but that didn't make sense.

They were all dead.

I dumped everything in the washer and turned the knob to start it. Time to clean the kitchen. I better clean the kitchen. The kitchen needs to be cleaned.

The part of me clinging to my sanity tried to slap me out of my shock. But the slap wasn't hard enough to register, and I no longer cared . . . about anything.

The right side of my ribs banged into the countertop as I fumbled around the kitchen. The table appeared to hold the biggest mess, well, next to all the blood. Papers and receipts covered most of the surface, but it was the scroll the witches had left us that caught my attention.

I lifted the rolled up pieces to my nose and took a whiff, filtering through the other aromas fused into the thick paper until I found Larissa's scent. My nose remembered it the moment my delicate senses reached it. She reeked of licorice and sunflowers, of all things. A unique blend. Too unique. Easy to find.

I tucked the parchment beneath my arm and I shoved my bare feet into a pair of sneakers Shayna had abandoned near the foyer. A laugh I hadn't expected broke through my hoarse throat, mixing with the sniffles that continued to irritate my nose. Shayna wouldn't need her ratty canvas shoes anymore, would she?

I sighed, staring back at the mess in my house. But

it would have to wait. It wasn't time to clean, or scrub, or tidy up.

It was time to hunt.

Chapter Ten

Protection. The last challenge. The one I catastrophically misinterpreted.

This whole damn thing had been about me, at least at first. Beast. I was one. Self. I fought me. Protection . . . I didn't need to protect me. I needed to protect *them*. And I failed. God, had I failed.

My sweat-soaked palms slicked the steering wheel. I struggled to keep our Subaru on the road. My nerves wouldn't allow me to focus, and my tigress could already taste Larissa's blood.

I wiped my clammy cheeks and concentrated on the stretch of highway ahead. The last time I'd spoken to Danny, he'd mentioned that members of the clan supposedly gathered around Meeks Bay to practice making it rain this time of year. I hadn't construed it as useful information then, but now it seemed helpful—valuable even. Perhaps one of the witches would lead me to Larissa if I asked politely.

Or not so politely.

If I thought about it, Meeks Bay provided the perfect location for a bewitching rendezvous during the winter months. In the summer, hordes of campers would rent out the surrounding cabins or spend the day lounging on the beach. In February, tourists were too busy skiing their way down the mountains of Squaw Valley. It should be deserted for the most part in winter. Good. I didn't need an audience, not for what I planned to do.

The afternoon clouds shadowed the lake as I drove along 89, while birds hurried to return to their shelters as the heavy snowfall began. I wondered if Saint Peter would reunite me with my sisters tonight, or if he would find me unworthy of entrance into heaven. "Thou shall not kill, remember?" a voice reminded me. But did God make exceptions for those so sick with grief they could barely stay within the yellow lines?

I guess I'll find out.

I pulled into The Wild Willow, Meeks Bay's resort and the sole camp rental facility in the area. The two-story clapboard building had closed down for the winter, but for the moment, it remained my only lead. I drove through the lot and over the wide snowy lawn, steering the Legacy behind a thick cluster of trees. I cut the engine and waited, not bothering to leave the heat on. It didn't take long for the falling snow to cover my tracks, or my windshield. But I didn't need to see, only hear. Hear for any sounds of voices, or steps, or breaths.

Muffled yells of my sisters jolted my already fragile nerves. And at one point I thought I felt Emme's touch. I closed my eyes and allowed one more tear to fall before I reached for my predator's hunger. My stomach growled. I needed to eat. I wondered briefly how Larissa would taste.

I didn't know how Larissa had managed to take my sisters from me, but the longer I sat against the chilly leather seat, the more I realized how much I'd miss them. It had only been the four of us for so long. And while I knew their future spouses and families would eventually sever our close-knit bond, I hadn't prepared myself to lose them so soon. I'd thought for sure we had a few good years left. Now, we didn't have anything.

Blackness claimed the inside of the car. In the darkness, my sisters' cries pleaded with me to return home. But all that awaited me were their corpses. I didn't want to view their dead bodies again so soon.

Or ever.

I heard a set of tires crunch through the snow near the front of the building, followed quickly by another set. The voices were mere whispers and far from where I hid. Still I heard them.

Someone opened a car door. "Don't worry. You can't see our cars from the road."

Doors slammed shut. "It's freezing," a different person said.

"Quit complaining," another snapped. "And hurry up. We have to replace the other group before Larissa gets pissed."

Bingo.

I waited until the footsteps all but faded from my sensitive ears before stepping out. Snow fell onto my hair and bare arms and my warm breath filled the night. I jerked, as if jolted, and scanned the area, searching for the witches. Nothing there. The group was getting further away. I needed to move. Now.

My tigress kept our steps light. I veered around the corner where three Jettas had parked in an old stable area serving as a carport. The witches were right; no way would their cars be visible from the road. But I wasn't hunting Jettas. I was hunting their drivers.

I stayed low, following the fresh footsteps across the street. When I neared the trail leading to rental cottages, I slipped into the woods. I barely sensed the snow drifting into my shoes and soaking my tank top. I ignored the goosebumps spreading up my arms and the inadvertent shakes of my body. Instead, I focused on the aromas of mint, rosemary, saffron, and nutmeg the witches emitted like a spice rack. The four witches I followed had abandoned their Gap clothes and replaced them with red medieval capes. They resembled liquid fire as the wind fluttered their capes against the white wilderness.

None appeared to notice me. They kept their heads down against the increasing wind, and their conversation revolved around the miserable weather. I kept my distance, ducking low into the brush where the trees thinned out. They couldn't sense my magic from this far away. At least, that's what I counted on.

I'd taken several careful paces when I thought I heard Taran swearing from somewhere far behind me. I glanced back. Only the outstretched limbs of barren trees greeted me. Not the arms of my sisters. Of course not the arms of my sisters. My tigress chuffed, imploring me to concentrate on the task. I veered back and continued my chase.

After about fifteen minutes of trudging through and griping about the snow, the witches came upon an old mountain cabin shaped like a giant wooden triangle. There were three levels; the top had two windows and was swathed in complete darkness—likely a small loft. Only one lamp lit the second floor. Candles flickered on the first, but the drapes kept me from seeing more than a few figures pacing. They didn't, however, keep me from hearing the muted chants of the coven.

"Find her," one woman called.

"Find her," the group repeated.

"Guide her."

"Guide her."

"Blind her."

"Blind her."

"See through only us. We implore you."

"See through only us. We implore you."

One of the witches knocked on the door. "Dearest of

sisters, the coven of four seeks entrance."

The spiky-haired witch who'd written the F-you scroll answered the door. "Good noon, sisters. Thank you for coming. Please hurry, our other sisters grow weary."

They entered without looking back. That was their first mistake. I prowled toward the front only to smack face first into an invisible shield, several yards from the front steps.

Shit.

I pressed against it. It felt as slick as glass, but as thick as the kind that separates tellers from would-be bank robbers. My hands slid to the bottom and my claws dug deep into the snow. Whatever defense they used seemed to extend into the ground. But how far down?

One way to find out.

I *shifted* as far deep as I could and then across. I didn't know if the safeguard they used could slice me, dice me, burn me, or melt me. But I planned to die anyway, so it didn't make much difference. I surfaced just in front of the warped wooden steps, trying to slow my gasps so they weren't so audible. In the end, my efforts didn't help.

"What was that?" someone new asked.

I leapt onto the steps, impatient with the need to act. I punched my fists through the door, yanked it off its hinges, and launched it into the force field with the strength of my grief. The oak door wedged into the shield. From the base, a long crack shot high into the sky like a reverse bolt of red lightning. Three women screamed and collapsed to the floor. I supposed their magic had fed the shield. They should have done a better job.

I jumped over them as I stalked my way inside.

Chapter Eleven

The stunned faces of ten witches greeted me. With the exception of a few chairs and a table, the large open room sat bare. A pentacle had been carved into the wide-plank floorboards. Five witches sat at each point with their staffs and talismans between them. In the center of the star lay four pictures of me and my three dead sisters. A kitchen knife crossed over Shayna's photo, and a small bottle of what reeked of nightshade rested over Emme's. Taran's, of course, came complete with a noose made from ribbon. The eyes in my photo had been blacked out with a marker. Strands of my left-over hair bound each one.

They'd used the bloodline I shared with my sisters to reach them. That's how they'd killed them. I'd been part of their weapon. The knowledge fueled my fury like a gasoline-powered inferno. They should have hidden that little tidbit from me. Now I knew. Now they'd pay.

The four witches I'd followed and the spiky-haired witch watched slack-jawed as I marched into the pentacle. The edges popped and sizzled when I stepped through. It seemed my physical presence broke their spell.

I bent and lifted each photo. The murder weapons

slipped off as I raised the images to my face. It appeared they'd spent the days before the attacks following us, or hired a human to do it. Otherwise I would have sensed their magic.

Shayna's picture showed her laughing. She'd always had the best smile and personality. Emme's depicted her shyness, by showing her head slightly lowered. Taran scowled in her picture as she analyzed a box of cereal. I remembered that day. We'd gone to the market. She'd complained how expensive food was in the Tahoe region. The one of me had Emme's head resting against my shoulder. I couldn't see her face, but her light strands were unmistakable. She readily demonstrated affection that way. Would I ever feel her head against me again?

No.

I held the pictures with great care, remembering the last days we'd spent together. But then the memories of our last few hours dug their way through the numbness and shot through like an eruption of lava. My eyes skimmed along the five making up the circle. "*Run,*" I growled. "*Run for your lives.*"

They stumbled to their feet, tripping over their long skirts in their haste. A few of them grabbed their now semi-conscious members and yanked them to their feet and out the door. The first one to escape screamed for Genevieve. That's okay. I'd take her on next. But first . . .

The large oak table smashed to splinters in front of Spiky and the four witches I'd tracked. They'd tried to follow suit behind the rest of their coven. But they needed to stay. My tigress eyes met Spiky's, forcing her already fair skin to whiten to chalk. "Uh, uh. Not you. Where's Larissa?"

She lifted her chin in a show of force. Maybe it would have worked if she'd met my gaze, or if perspiration hadn't formed across her brow, or if the aroma of her fear hadn't riled the thirst of my beast. "You don't know who you're dealing with."

The one whose staff I'd thrown into the street charged me. She lifted the long wooden stick with a banshee scream and pointed it directly at my heart. Light from her amber stone filled the room with yellow and drenched the air with nauseating magic. "*Fue—*"

I cut off her spell by snatching her staff from her hands, snapping it in two, and jamming the sharp end into her thigh.

She crumpled against the floor, wailing.

Stupid bitch should have learned the first time. I separated the amber stone from the tip of the staff and tossed it into a fireplace made from river rocks. "Anyone else?" They exchanged glances, but didn't speak. "Where's Larissa?" I hissed again over the pained cries of their sister.

Their silence made me impatient. I kicked the howling woman at my feet into the two witches closest to me when they drew their magic. The three of them slammed into the wall, denting the sheetrock. Poor wall.

The witches fell forward in a mound of groaning bodies, except for the one with the piece of staff jutting from her thigh. She continued to scream. They half-crawled, half-staggered out the door, joining the others who beseeched Genevieve to appear. Two witches left. I only needed one to summon Larissa.

But then I didn't even need one. The sound of sliding fabric had me veering toward the worn wooden steps. Larissa's bare foot, the one with the amethyst toe rings, appeared at the landing. They sparkled with lavender light and heat as they paused before taking the next step. She knew I was here. And why I'd arrived. She took another step, followed by another, until her curvy figure presented itself. Her tight blond curls stuck to her face. She fluffed them with her fingers with casual grace.

She'd been sleeping. My sisters were dead and she'd been sleeping.

I thought back to the pentacle. The efforts of the challenges must have drained her. Hell, they'd drained me. Had she put her clan in charge of maintaining them? Was that even legal? Too bad I didn't care enough to ask. The outcome remained the same. She was going to die—or I would, trying to kill her.

The edges of her long, gray velvet dress dragged along the steps. She barely acknowledged me as she swept into the kitchen where a few bottles of wine and bottled water sat in a neat little row. She poured herself a glass of red. Although she kept her back to me, I wasn't stupid enough to think she couldn't see me attack. The newt incident had taught me that much.

Larissa took a sip. "Mmm. Good year." She took another sip. Then she finally looked at me. "What's wrong, Celia? Rough day?"

I didn't feel my legs bend into a crouch or propel me forward, but suddenly I was airborne with my front claws extended toward Larissa's throat. I'd grazed her jugular when I stopped moving, frozen in air. Rays of purple light from her toe rings flickered below me and sent a heat wave to warm my belly. Her magic had saved her. This time.

Larissa clutched her throat as a stream of red seeped through her fingers. She hadn't expected me to move so fast. And neither had I.

The witches near the door gasped. Larissa ducked under my reach, not that it mattered. I could barely breathe, let alone move. She ripped a kitchen towel off a hook to pat her throat, then stared at the bloody cloth. Her scowl met my furious glare. "You were supposed to cry *misericordia* long before this." Her tone made me think my lack of dying bothered her.

Sucked to be her.

Her head whirled toward the spiky-haired witch. "Did the others maintain my spell?"

Spiky nodded. "Yes, Sister Larissa. All day." She glanced my way. "Just like you demanded of us. But maintaining the intensity of the *velum* drained their strength." She motioned to me with a nod. "They lost Celia and couldn't find her."

"That's because *she* came to find *you*. You're all weak!" Larissa wiped her neck in rapid strokes. A heavy lavender mist formed around her throat. When she removed her hand, my claw marks had vanished.

The other witch stepped forward. Her straight auburn hair angled in a bob along her narrow chin. "If it doesn't offend, Sister Larissa, why did you insist the others maintain your spell, especially if you consider them so weak?" She glanced my way, careful to avoid my stare. "This was your challenge alone to bear."

Larissa dropped her bloody rag on the floor and slowly snaked her way to the witch who spoke. Her bare feet slapped against the old wood with purpose and rage. She wanted to draw blood, possibly from one of her clan. I could sense the menace boiling to the surface in the way her rings painted the hem of her skirt a deep purple. The auburn-haired witch surprised me by not bowing when Larissa circled her. She wasn't fearful of Larissa. If anything, she appeared disgusted.

Larissa narrowed her eyes. She didn't seem to appreciate her inferior's lack of panic. "It does offend." She shoved her face into her subordinate's. "And as your leader, I may use you as I see fit."

The witch kept her gaze straight. "Genevieve won't approve. The challenge isn't just—"

Larissa smacked her hard across the face. The witch's head flew back. She blinked several times as the print of Larissa's hand swelled against her cheek.

"Genevieve doesn't lead you!" Larissa screamed at her.

The other witch said no more. Larissa left her and

returned to me. "Now, where were we?" Flames shot out high from the stove like a grease fire. "Oh, yes. I do believe you owe me a plea of mercy."

The auburn-haired witch stumbled forward. "That's four challenges!" she hollered. When Larissa ignored her, the auburn-haired witch raced out the door, joining the other witches now shrieking for Genevieve to appear.

The entire house rattled as lightning struck outside, bursting like fire against the windows. The witches bellowed their summoning chant, imploring Genevieve to appear. Screams replaced soft voices. Accusations turned to sobs. And something cracked and splintered like glass.

I didn't care, not about them or their damn drama. Larissa had destroyed everyone I'd loved. She needed to bleed and I needed to make it happen. If only I could break from her grasp.

Larissa angled my body around in a semi-circle so my face would be the first to meet the blaze. My back bowed and arched. The spell Larissa had wielded to kill my sisters had obviously drained her. Her power was fading fast, only not fast enough. She inched me closer to the stove. Fire licked the edges of my hair, smoking and curling the ends. Sweat and tears dripped down my chin. I bucked and thrashed, still unable to move my arms as if bound. But my legs? They'd always ruled as my strongest part.

Larissa took another sip of wine as she lowered me another few inches. "Say it, Celia. Just say it and this all ends."

The back of my foot connected with her wine glass. It shattered against her face. She screamed, releasing me from her magical grasp.

The force of my kick swerved me enough so only my arm hit the stove. The flames had extinguished from Larissa's lack of focus, but the metal grills seared my arm like a piece of fish, flaking off chunks of my flesh. I grunted, clenching my jaw from the wretched sting, refusing to scream. Larissa had caused me enough pain. I wouldn't allow her the pleasure of witnessing more. I wrenched away from the stove, just as the rising power of Larissa's magic showered the kitchen with lavender light.

I threw myself across the wooden floor, narrowly missing the avocado green refrigerator she launched in my direction. It broke against the wall, barely shuddering when she attempted to draw it back.

"*Bitch!*" she screamed. Blood oozed from her right eye and from a gash across her nose. But there was no time to heal. After all, she had a tigress to deal with.

I kicked up into a standing position and growled. My claws slowly protruded through my fingertips as I made my way toward my prey. The dishwasher hurtled from the wall. I leapt over it easily, its speed no match for mine. I focused on Larissa with predator eyes, trailing her as she backed away.

"Celia?"

Taran's gargled voice halted my steps. What felt like a bucket of slush chilled my skin. My breath quickened. *She shouldn't be here.*

"Ceel? Celia, please look at me."

She shouldn't be here!

I rammed my eyes shut and buried my pain deep. The cool air in the kitchen shifted. I opened my lids in time to dive out of the way of a flying chair. My claws dug into floor as Taran's four-inch sandals stepped in front of me. Her legs held that same sickly green tone. I shot to my feet, grinding my fangs to keep from screaming. Bruised marks coiled around her neck. Only the whites of her eyes showed. She smiled without humor. "Don't hurt her, Ceel." She scraped a long manicured fingertip across the note still pinned to her white nightgown. "I told you. It's my fault."

I clutched her cold body against me, trembling. My eyes stung. "It's not. I failed you."

Emme's voice replaced Taran's. "We forgive you, Celia."

I held her at arm's length. Emme's soft green eyes barely registered my face. Her mouth opened, spilling white foam. She gagged and choked. I lifted her in my arms and lay her on the floor on her side. As I pushed the hair out of her face, her blond, wavy strands transformed into Shayna's black silk locks beneath my fingertips. Shayna curled into the knife still imbedded in her sternum. Dark clots leeched out of her mouth as the bloodstain around her chest widened. My hands wandered over her body, desperate to help her, yet unsure how.

Something solid broke against my skull. I flew backwards and landed hard on my spine. My vision cleared in time to see Shayna jerk the knife from her sternum and plunge it down toward my chest. I clutched her wrist with one hand. Whoever she was, whatever she was, didn't stand a chance against the strength of a four-hundred pound predator. I shoved my feet into her stomach and thrust, sending her soaring into the pentacle.

She hovered above the sacred circle as it electrified like live wire, disintegrating my hair and the pictures into dust. Shayna's thin, bloody frame twitched and jerked, turning into Emme, then Taran, then Shayna once more before vanishing in a mushroom cloud of lavender.

Lavender.

Larissa.

God damn her!

I rushed to my feet, swerving out of the path of chairs, wine bottles, and appliances jetting at me in a purple haze. I used my brute strength to catch the speeding microwave and launched it back at Larissa. It hit her hard in the stomach and sent her sprawling back against the cabinets. Blood squirted from her eye, forming a puddle of ooze. She whimpered, trying desperately to rid herself of the microwave against her lap. Time was up. Five steps to go until she died.

A misshapen chair cracked me hard across my knee. I fell against my seared arm. The blisters that had formed burst opened and the raw skin scraped against the splintering floor. I roared, in fury and in anguish.

My head snapped up in the direction of the attack. The green talisman around Spiky's neck glimmered as she levitated the chair she'd struck me with over my head. It sparkled with the power of her mysticism. Turned out she had a pair after all. Except her last-ditch efforts weren't enough to save her. I hurled a discarded water canister into her face. It bounced off her forehead, but she didn't bounce off the floor when she landed. She fell face first like a wet sponge. The chair crashed next to me, its leg smashing my hand. I shook off the crushing pain. My job wasn't done. Larissa still lived.

Tentative hands reached in and pulled Spiky's unconscious form through the bent door frame as I tried to rise. My kneecap rested somewhere to the far right of where it should have been and the swelling told me moving was a very bad idea. But not moving was even worse. My hands gripped the edge of the counter and pulled. I managed to stand and straighten my left leg. I limped forward, ignoring the throbbing pain in my leg, the burning of my arm, and the crushed bones in my hand.

Larissa groaned as she finally shoved the microwave off her lap. I should have thanked her. It made it easier for me to dig the claws of my uninjured hand into her throat and yank her to her feet. We stared at each other, long and hard, as we both panted. Few beings had ever managed to keep my gaze. It should have unnerved me, but then again Larissa was a predator in her own right.

Larissa's magically reinforced foot sputtered and crackled, sending tiny sparks against my exposed shins. I barely felt it. The nap she'd taken before I'd arrived hadn't been enough to reenergize her. My head angled toward her, and my beast surged forward. And still Larissa kept her eyes on mine.

"Go ahead," she spat. "I'm not afraid to die."

And she wasn't. Maybe that was part of her problem.

The kill would be so easy. Blood from where my claws pierced her neck already drenched my hand. Another minor squeeze and I'd crush her larynx. The swelling alone would suffocate her. And she'd die slowly. I could even watch if I wanted to. Watch her irises dilate with fear as her body fought to take a breath. Watch her clutch her throat, or flail her arms, or . . .

My grasp loosened. In the end, no matter what I did, it wouldn't bring back Shayna's smile, Emme's soft touch, or Taran's fiery spirit.

Just like my first kills hadn't brought back our parents.

Larissa didn't value the gift of life. What she'd done to my family proved as much. She did love one thing, probably almost as much as I loved my sisters. The claws of my foot shot through the threadbare canvas of my sneakers. Larissa's lids peeled back as I dug them into her toes. I ignored the screaming muscles of my injured leg and punctured through the tiny bones of her foot. She screeched, sobbing *misericordia* over and over again until I kicked my foot back.

Her toes and the amethyst encrusted rings rolled in separate directions across the floor. I released Larissa then. She slid along the wall, her eyes wide and her cries strangely childlike. She gripped her dripping foot while I quietly gathered her former source of power. As I bent to pick up the rings, I thought about where I should go. Danny would come help me if I asked. He probably would even stay and watch over the house until it was sold. Me? I needed to leave. There was nothing here for me anymore.

The soft brush of a skirt made me glance up.

Genevieve had finally arrived. Her lithe body strode in with her long dark hair sweeping behind her. Once more she kept her long staff against her side. I thought she resembled a vampire when I first saw her. Now she appeared more like an angel. A fallen angel. Had she come to claim me?

A group of her witches gathered in the doorway. "Leave us," Genevieve told them. They paused before turning their backs and walking down the steps. A few glanced back. Their wary faces told me they didn't want to leave her alone with the scary beast.

Genevieve's large blue eyes blinked back at me with a hint of sadness as she scanned my wobbly form. "You've been through a lot," she said softly.

My voice cracked at her acknowledgement. "I guess you can say that."

Her gaze dropped to the toe rings in the palm of my broken hand. "May I?"

Before I could answer, or think to protect them, Genevieve called forth her magic. Her long wooden staff radiated a bright yellow light, similar to the warm summer sun yet gentle against my eyes. She blew a soft breath onto the rings. Just like that they disintegrated to ash.

Larissa stopped wailing, realizing Tahoe had a new head witch.

Genevieve regarded me closely. "You won the challenge, Celia." She glimpsed at Larissa. "No matter how unjust the obstacles." She watched me carefully when I didn't answer. "Forgive me for not arriving sooner. Larissa used her power to block my sisters' calls."

I nodded, but still refused to answer. Genevieve reached to touch my shoulder except thought better of it when she caught my scowl. Just because she destroyed a few rings without taking out the entire structure didn't mean I trusted her. "Will you give us a week, to gather our things?"

I barely understood her words. "Huh?"

Genevieve smiled patiently. "The conditions of winning the challenge oblige us to leave the area."

She was right. My victory entitled me to banish them forever. They wanted to stay near Tahoe. The lake represented everything they worshipped—nature and magic in one lovely, almighty source. Denying them would rob them of something beautiful and sacred. Just as I'd been robbed. But hurting them wouldn't end my pain or alleviate my sorrow. Part of me wanted them to suffer, to continue suffering. The other part of me that wanted to reunite with my family knew my soul needed closure.

I shook my head. "You don't have to leave. You can stay if you'd like. I just want to be left in peace." I swallowed the lump in my throat. "That's all we, I mean, *I* ever wanted."

Genevieve bowed her head slightly. "Thank you, Celia. Thank you. And of course, I'll see to it that you and your sisters are left alone—"

My glare cut her words like a knife. Genevieve took a step back, gripping her staff against her. Rage boiled my blood like water. "My *sisters*? I don't have any sisters!"

Genevieve's lips parted. "Oh, my God."

Once more, the muffled sound of my sibling's voices haunted my thoughts. Genevieve's brows raised with shock—no, not shock, more like surprise. Surprise that I didn't know . . .

My sisters' voices grew louder, clearer. "What's a *velum*?" I asked, suddenly remembering.

"Pardon?"

My breath came out in a shudder. "The witches said they had trouble maintaining the intensity of Larissa's *velum*. What is that?"

Genevieve clasped a hand over her mouth. "You really don't know, do you?"

"Just tell me what it is!"

Genevieve dropped her hand and sighed. "It's a veil,

CECY ROBSON

Celia. A very powerful, very graphic, very cruel veil."

Everything went still. I stopped breathing, not wanting to believe what my logic was screaming at me. The newt. The image of myself. Physical and real to some extent, but mostly . . . an illusion.

Genevieve took a cautious step toward me. "They're alive, Celia. Your sisters are alive. They're waiting for you outside."

I stumbled forward, slapping Genevieve's hand away when she tried to steady me. I hobbled as fast as my legs could carry me, falling against the porch railing. The coven screamed collectively, struggling to maintain the newly restored force field.

It stood no chance against my sisters.

My family reeled behind it, bashing it with the might of their combined power, dressed in the clothes they'd slept in. Shayna hacked through the clear barrier like wood, screaming at the witches holding it in place. Taran's entire body glowed in blue and white flame, melting through the shield. Her swears and threats were muffled, but as beautiful as a dove's song to my ears. Even Emme, my sweet little Emme, was enraged. Her *force* peeled away the sections Shayna chopped. They'd smash through in seconds. But the seconds were too long to wait. I bolted toward them, pushing past the pain and the witches blocking my path.

"Release the barricade," Genevieve ordered.

The witches collapsed as I reached for my sisters. Three sets of arms gathered me to them, wrapping me tightly in their strength and love.

I sobbed. With all that I had, for all that I had, I sobbed.

87

Chapter Twelve

Emme leaned across the table, wrinkling the crisp white linen. "D-do you think Genevieve killed Larissa?"

She had waited for our server to leave with our food order before asking. Around us, the patrons of the posh bistro engaged in quiet, polite conversations about the events of the day, not life-harrowing events involving real-life wicked witches and newts the size of Subarus.

I thought about how Genevieve slipped back into the house and darkened the doorway and windows with her own veil. Just before Larissa's screams began. My finger traced down the stem of my water glass. "Maybe. But it's none of our business, and I really don't care."

"Neither do I," Taran muttered. "And neither should you, Emme."

Four days had passed since the last challenge. I'd told my sisters Larissa had feigned their deaths, but I wouldn't discuss the details. Emme's healing touch had mended my physical wounds and soothed my emotional ones enough to allow me to sleep. But the *velum* had been powerful. It would take time for the images to completely fade, especially since they'd manifested from my deepest fears.

"So what happened?" I asked. My emotional breakdown at Meek's Bay had made them tiptoe around me. They'd told me very little, waiting, I guessed, until I was ready to discuss things. "When I was at the house?"

Shayna and Emme looked to Taran. She shrugged and adjusted the wristwatch I'd bought her for her birthday. It was a gesture she often did when she didn't want to deal with the intensity of her emotions. "I woke up to you tearing my closet apart. I asked what you were doing, but you didn't seem to be able to hear me." She shook her head slowly. "But your face— Shit, Ceel, you looked whiter than death. You kept, I don't know, acting things out. When I tried to grab you, my hands went right through you, like you weren't really there . . . or no longer real." She pursed her lips. "I called to Emme and Shayna, but they couldn't figure out what was wrong, either."

My glance shot across the table to Shayna. "You weren't in the kitchen making breakfast?"

Shayna raised her brows. "No. I'd gone to bed late keeping watch. I was still sleeping when Taran started yelling. You kept saying things, but we couldn't hear you. And like Taran said, you couldn't hear us. We followed you into the kitchen then up to Emme's room. We tried to grab you, slap you—Emme even tried to hold you with her *force*. Nothing worked. We thought for sure you were, like, *gone*."

The waiter dropped off our drinks. "Your meals will be ready shortly." He jumped when he caught my expression. Shayna smiled reassuringly at him until he inched away to the next table.

Emme's hand covered mine. "You were so upset. It broke our hearts to see you hurting. And we knew it was bad, but we didn't understand the extent of your pain." Her eyes reddened. "I'm so sorry, Celia."

I turned over my hand and gave her small fingers a

squeeze. "What else happened?"

Taran tapped her French-tipped nails against the table. "After playing with the phone you started cleaning. At first we thought you found a way out of the spell you'd been placed in and were coming back to us. But then you found the scroll. And Ceel, that's when a whole new kind of scary beast unleashed. We jumped in the car with you. Shayna barely managed to drag Emme in before you sped off." She huffed. "We didn't have coats or anything. You drove us to the bay and we spent the next two hours screaming and trying to get your attention. You didn't even blink when I zapped you with lightning."

Shayna gulped her water. "It wasn't until you jumped out of the car and we spotted the Jettas that we knew what was happening. But then we lost you in the woods when Taran twisted her ankle. Once Emme healed her, it took us a while to find you through the storm. The snow clouded everything. Taran couldn't pick up on the witch mojo and your steps were barely traceable."

Emme smiled softly. "When we finally found you the shield was up. But it doesn't look like you needed us after all."

I rubbed my eyes, trying to stay calm and not think about how I almost lost them. "Trust me. I need you. All of you."

Shayna grinned. "We need you, too, dude. You saved our butts and kicked Larissa's in the process." She raised her glass. "To Celia."

"To our beautiful home," Emme added.

"To staying out of trouble," Taran muttered.

I would have believed her. I wanted to believe her. If only she hadn't winked at the vampire seated across from us...

Read on as the Weird Girls saga continues with *Sealed with a Curse,* the first full length novel in The Weird Girls Urban Fantasy Romance series by Cecy Robson. The excerpt has been set for this edition only and may not reflect the final content of the final novel.

Sealed with a Curse

A Weird Girls Novel

By

CECY ROBSON

Chapter One

Sacramento, California

The courthouse doors crashed open as I led my three sisters into the large foyer. I didn't mean to push so hard, but hell, I was mad and worried about being eaten. The cool spring breeze slapped at my back as I stepped inside, yet it did little to cool my temper or my nerves.

My nose scented the vampires before my eyes caught them emerging from the shadows. There were six of them, wearing dark suits, Ray-Bans, and obnoxious little grins. Two bolted the doors tight behind us, while the others frisked us for weapons.

I can't believe we we're in vampire court. So much for avoiding the perilous world of the supernatural.

Emme trembled beside me. She had every right to be scared. We were strong, but our combined abilities couldn't trump a roomful of bloodsucking beasts. "Celia," she whispered, her voice shaking. "Maybe we shouldn't have come."

Like we had a choice. "Just stay close to me, Emme." My muscles tensed as the vampire's hands swept the length of my body and through my long curls. I didn't like him touching me, and neither did my inner tigress. My fingers itched with the need to protrude my claws.

When he finally released me, I stepped closer to Emme while I scanned the foyer for a possible escape route. Next to me, the vampire searching Taran got a little daring with his pat-down. But he was messing with the wrong sister.

"If you touch my ass one more time, fang boy, I swear to God I'll light you on fire." The vampire quickly removed his hands when a spark of blue flame ignited from Taran's fingertips.

Shayna, conversely, flashed a lively smile when the vampire searching her found her toothpicks. Her grin widened when he returned her seemingly harmless little sticks, unaware of how deadly they were in her hands. "Thanks, dude." She shoved the box back into the pocket of her slacks.

"They're clear." The guard grinned at Emme and licked his lips. "This way." He motioned her to follow. Emme cowered. Taran showed no fear and plowed ahead. She tossed her dark, wavy hair and strutted into the courtroom like the diva she was, wearing a tiny white mini dress that contrasted with her deep olive skin. I didn't fail to notice the guards' gazes glued to Taran's shapely figure. Nor did I miss when their incisors lengthened, ready to bite.

I urged Emme and Shayna forward. "Go. I'll watch your backs." I whipped around to snarl at the guards. The vampires' smiles faltered when they saw *my* fangs protrude. Like most beings, they probably didn't know what I was, but they seemed to recognize that I was potentially lethal, despite my petite frame.

I followed my sisters into the large courtroom. The place reminded me of a picture I'd seen of the Salem witch trials. Rows of dark wood pews lined the center aisle, and wide rustic planks comprised the floor. Unlike the photo I recalled, every window was boarded shut, and paintings of vampires hung on every inch of available wall space. One particular image epitomized the vampire stereotype perfectly. It showed a male vampire entwined with two naked women on a bed of roses and jewels. The women appeared completely enamored of the vampire, even while blood dripped from their necks.

The vampire spectators scrutinized us as we approached along the center aisle. Many had accessorized their expensive attire with diamond jewelry and watches that probably cost more than my car. Their glares told me they didn't appreciate my cotton T-shirt, peasant skirt, and flip-flops. I was twenty-five years old; it's not like I didn't know how to dress. But, hell, other fabrics and shoes were way more expensive to replace when I *changed* into my other form.

I spotted our accuser as we stalked our way to the front of the assembly. Even in a courtroom crammed with young and sexy vampires, Misha Aleksandr stood out. His tall, muscular frame filled his fitted suit, and his long blond hair brushed against his shoulders. Death, it seemed, looked damn good. Yet it wasn't his height or his wealth or even his striking features that captivated me. He possessed a fierce presence that commanded the room. Misha Aleksandr was a force to be reckoned with, but, strangely enough, so was I.

Misha had "requested" our presence in Sacramento after charging us with the murder of one of his family members. We had two choices: appear in court or be hunted for the rest of our lives. The whole situation sucked. We'd stayed hidden from the supernatural world for so long. Now not only had we been forced into the limelight, but we also faced the possibility of dying some twisted, Rob Zombie–inspired death.

Of course, God forbid that would make Taran shut her trap. She leaned in close to me. "Celia, how about I gather some magic-borne sunlight and fry these assholes?" she whispered in Spanish.

A few of the vampires behind us muttered and hissed, causing uproar among the rest. If they didn't like us before, they sure as hell hated us then.

Shayna laughed nervously, but maintained her perky demeanor. "I think some of them understand the lingo, dude."

I recognized Taran's desire to burn the vamps to blood and ash, but I didn't agree with it. Conjuring such power would leave her drained and vulnerable, easy prey for the master vampires, who would be immune to her sunlight. Besides, we were already in trouble with one master for killing his keep. We didn't need to be hunted by the entire leeching species.

The procession halted in a strangely wide-open area before a raised dais. There were no chairs or tables, nothing we could use as weapons against the judges or the angry mob amassed behind us.

My eyes focused on one of the boarded windows. The light honey-colored wood frame didn't match the darker boards. I guessed the last defendant had tried to escape. Judging from the claw marks running from beneath the frame to where I stood, he, she, or *it* hadn't made it.

I looked up from the deeply scratched floor to find Misha's intense gaze on me. We locked eyes, predator to predator, neither of us the type to back down. *You're trying to intimidate the wrong gal, pretty boy. I don't scare easily.*

Shayna slapped her hand over her face and shook her head, her long black ponytail waving behind her. "For Pete's sake, Celia, can't you be a little friendlier?" She flashed Misha a grin that made her blue eyes sparkle. "How's it going, dude?"

Shayna said "dude" a lot, ever since dating some idiot claiming to be a professional surfer. The term fit her sunny personality and eventually grew on us.

Misha didn't appear taken by her charm. He eyed her

as if she'd asked him to make her a garlic pizza in the shape of a cross. I laughed; I couldn't help it. *Leave it to Shayna to try to befriend the guy who'll probably suck us dry by sundown.*

At the sound of my chuckle, Misha regarded me slowly. His head tilted slightly as his full lips curved into a sensual smile. I would have preferred a vicious stare—I knew how to deal with those. For a moment, I thought he'd somehow made my clothes disappear and I was standing there like the bleeding hoochies in that awful painting.

The judges' sudden arrival gave me an excuse to glance away. There were four, each wearing a formal robe of red velvet with an elaborate powdered wig. They were probably several centuries old, but like all vampires, they didn't appear a day over thirty. Their splendor easily surpassed the beauty of any mere mortal. I guessed the whole "sucky, sucky, me love you all night" lifestyle paid off for them.

The judges regally assumed their places on the raised dais. Behind them hung a giant plasma screen, which appeared out of place in this century-old building. Did they plan to watch a movie while they decided how best to disembowel us?

A female judge motioned Misha forward with a Queen Elizabeth hand wave. A long, thick scar angled from the corner of her left jaw across her throat. Someone had tried to behead her. To scar a vampire like that, the culprit had likely used a gold blade reinforced with lethal magic. Apparently, even that blade hadn't been enough. I gathered she commanded the fang-fest Parliament, since her marble nameplate read, CHIEF JUSTICE ANTOINETTE MALIKA. Judge Malika didn't strike me as the warm and cuddly sort. Her lips were pursed into a tight line and her elongating fangs locked over her lower lip. I only hoped she'd snacked before her arrival.

At a nod from Judge Malika, Misha began. "Members

of the High Court, I thank you for your audience." A Russian accent underscored his deep voice. "I hereby charge Celia, Taran, Shayna, and Emme Wird with the murder of my family member, David Geller."

"Wird? More like *Weird*," a vamp in the audience mumbled. The smaller vamp next to him adjusted his bow tie nervously when I snarled.

Oh, yeah, like we've never heard that before, jerk.

The sole male judge slapped a heavy leather-bound book on the long table and whipped out a feather quill. "Celia Wird. State your position."

Position?

I exchanged glances with my sisters; they didn't seem to know what Captain Pointy Teeth meant either. Taran shrugged. "Who gives a shit? Just say something."

I waved a hand. "Um. Registered nurse?"

Judging by his "please don't make me eat you before the proceedings" scowl, and the snickering behind us, I hadn't provided him with the appropriate response.

He enunciated every word carefully and slowly so as to not further confuse my obviously feeble and inferior mind. "Position in the supernatural world."

"We've tried to avoid your world." I gave Taran the evil eye. "For the most part. But if you must know, I'm a tigress."

"Weretigress," he said as he wrote.

"I'm not a *were*," I interjected defensively.

He huffed. "Can you *change* into a tigress or not?"

"Well, yes. But that doesn't make me a *were*."

The vamps behind us buzzed with feverish whispers while the judges' eyes narrowed suspiciously. Not knowing what we were made them nervous. A nervous vamp was a dangerous vamp. And the room was bursting with them.

"What I mean is, unlike a *were*, I can *change* parts of my body without turning into my beast completely." And unlike anything else on earth, I could also *shift*—disappear under and across solid ground and resurface unscathed. But they didn't need to know that little tidbit. Nor did they need to know I couldn't heal my injuries. If it weren't for Emme's unique ability to heal herself and others, my sisters and I would have died long ago.

"Fascinating," he said in a way that clearly meant I wasn't. The feather quill didn't come with an eraser. And the judge obviously didn't appreciate my making him mess up his book. He dipped his pen into his little inkwell and scribbled out what he'd just written before addressing Taran. "Taran Wird, position?"

"I can release magic into the forms of fire and lightning—"

"Very well, witch." The vamp scrawled.

"I'm not a witch, asshole."

The judge threw his plume on the table, agitated. Judge Malika fixed her frown on Taran. "What did you say?"

Nobody flashed a vixen grin better than Taran. "I said, 'I'm not a witch. Ass. Hole.'"

Emme whimpered, ready to hurl from the stress. Shayna giggled and threw an arm around Taran. "She's just kidding, dude!"

No. Taran didn't kid. Hell, she didn't even know any knock-knock jokes. She shrugged off Shayna, unwilling to back down. She wouldn't listen to Shayna. But she would listen to me.

"Just answer the question, Taran."

The muscles on Taran's jaw tightened, but she did as I asked. "I make fire, light—"

"Fire-breather." Captain Personality wrote quickly.

"I'm not a—"

He cut her off. "Shayna Wird?"

"Well, dude, I throw knives—"

"Knife thrower," he said, ready to get this little meet-and-greet over and done with.

Shayna did throw knives. That was true. She could also transform pieces of wood into razor-sharp weapons and manipulate alloys. All she needed was metal somewhere on her body and a little focus. For her safety, though, "knife thrower" seemed less threatening.

"And you, Emme Wird?"

"Um. Ah. I can move things with my mind—"

"Gypsy," the half-wit interpreted.

I supposed "telekinetic" was too big a word for this idiot. Then again, unlike typical telekinetics, Emme could do more than bend a few forks. I sighed. *Tigress, fire-breather, knife thrower, and Gypsy.* We sounded like the headliners for a freak show. All we needed was a bearded lady. I sighed. *That's what happens when you're the bizarre products of a back-fired curse.*

Misha glanced at us quickly before stepping forward once more. "I will present Mr. Hank Miller and Mr. Timothy Brown as witnesses—" Taran exhaled dramatically and twirled her hair like she was bored. Misha glared at her before finishing. "I do not doubt justice will be served."

Judge Zhahara Nadim, who resembled more of an Egyptian queen than someone who should be stuffed into a powdered wig, surprised me by leering at Misha like she wanted his head for a lawn ornament. I didn't know what he'd done to piss her off; yet knowing we weren't the only ones hated brought me a strange sense of comfort. She narrowed her eyes at Misha, like all predators do before they strike, and called forward someone named "Destiny." I didn't know Destiny, but I knew she was no vampire the moment she strutted onto the dais.

I tried to remain impassive. However, I really wanted to run away screaming. Short of sporting a few tails and some extra digits, Destiny was the freakiest thing I'd ever seen. Not only did she lack the allure all vampires possessed, but her fashion sense bordered on disastrous.

She wore black patterned tights, white strappy sandals, and a hideous black-and-white polka-dot turtleneck. I guessed she sought to draw attention from her lime green zebra-print miniskirt. And, my God, her makeup was abominable. Black kohl outlined her bright fuchsia lips, and mint green shadow ringed her eyes.

"This is a perfect example of why I don't wear makeup," I told Taran.

Taran stepped forward with her hands on her hips. "How the hell is *she* a witness? I didn't see her at the club that night! And Lord knows she would've stuck out."

Emme trembled beside me. "Taran, please don't get us killed!"

I gave my youngest sister's hand a squeeze. "Steady, Emme."

Judge Malika called Misha's two witnesses forward. "Mr. Miller and Mr. Brown, which of you gentlemen would like to go first?"

Both "gentlemen" took one gander at Destiny and scrambled away from her. It was never a good sign when something scared a vampire. Hank, the bigger of the two vamps, shoved Tim forward.

"You may begin," Judge Malika commanded. "Just concentrate on what you saw that night. Destiny?"

The four judges swiftly donned protective earwear, like construction workers used, just as a guard flipped a switch next to the flat-screen. At first, I thought the judges toyed with us. Even with heightened senses, how could they hear the testimony through those ridiculous ear guards? Before I could protest, Destiny enthusiastically approached Tim and grabbed his head. Tim's immediate bloodcurdling screams caused the rest of us to cover our ears. Every hair on my body stood at attention. What freaked me out was that he wasn't the one on trial.

Emme's fair freckled skin blanched so severely, I feared she'd pass out. Shayna stood frozen with her jaw open while Taran and I exchanged "oh, shit" glances. I was about to start the "let's get the hell out of here" ball rolling when images from Tim's mind appeared on the screen. I couldn't believe my eyes. Complete with sound effects, we relived the night of David's murder. Misha straightened when he saw David soar out of Taran's window in flames, but otherwise he did not react. Nor did Misha blink when what remained of David burst into ashes on our lawn. Still, I sensed his fury. The image moved to a close-up of Hank's shocked face and finished with the four of us scowling down at the blood and ash.

Destiny abruptly released the sobbing Tim, who collapsed on the floor. Mucus oozed from his nose and mouth. I didn't even know vamps were capable of such body fluids.

At last, Taran finally seemed to understand the deep shittiness of our situation. "Son of a bitch," she whispered.

Hank gawked at Tim before addressing the judges. "If it pleases the court, I swear on my honor I witnessed exactly what Tim Brown did about David Geller's murder. My version would be of no further benefit."

Malika shrugged indifferently. "Very well, you're excused." She turned toward us while Hank hurried back to his seat. "As you just saw, we have ways to expose the truth. Destiny is able to extract memories, but she cannot alter them. Likewise, during Destiny's time with you, you will be unable to change what you saw. You'll only review what has already come to pass."

I frowned. "How do we know you're telling us the truth?"

Malika peered down her nose at me. "What choice do you have? Now, which of you is first?"

Reader's Guide to the Magical World of the Weird Girls Series

acute bloodlust A condition that occurs when a vampire goes too long without consuming blood. Increases the vampire's thirst to lethal levels. It is remedied by feeding the vampire.

Call The ability of one supernatural creature to reach out to another, through either thoughts or sounds. A vampire can pass his or her *call* by transferring a bit of magic into the receiving being's skin.

Change To transform from one being to another, typically from human to beast, and back again.

chronic bloodlust A condition caused by a curse placed on a vampire. It makes the vampire's thirst for blood insatiable and drives the vampire to insanity. The vampire grows in size from gluttony and assumes deformed features. There is no cure.

claim The method by which a werebeast consummates the union with his or her mate.

clan A group of werebeasts led by an Alpha. The types of clans differ depending on species. Werewolf clans are called "packs." Werelions belong to "prides."

Creatura The offspring of a demon lord and a werebeast.

dantem animam A soul giver. A rare being capable of returning a master vampire's soul. A master with a soul is more powerful than any other vampire in existence, as he or she is balancing life and death at once.

dark ones Creatures considered to be pure evil, such as shape-shifters or demons.

demon A creature residing in hell. Only the strongest demons may leave to stalk on earth, but their time is limited; the power of good compels them to return.

demon child The spawn of a demon lord and a mortal female. Demon children are of limited intelligence and rely predominantly on their predatory instincts.

demon lords (*demonkin*) The offspring of a witch mother and a demon. Powerful, cunning, and deadly. Unlike demons, whose time on earth is limited, demon lords may remain on earth indefinitely.

den A school where young werebeasts train and learn to fight in order to help protect the earth from mystical evil.

Elder One of the governors of a werebeast clan. Each clan is led by three Elders: an Alpha, a Beta, and an Omega. The Alpha is the supreme leader. The Beta is the second in command. The Omega settles disputes between them and has the ability to calm by releasing bits of his or her harmonized soul, or through a sense of humor muddled with magic. He possesses rare gifts and is often volatile, selfish, and of questionable loyalty.

force Emme Wird's ability to move objects with her mind.

gold The metallic element; it was cursed long ago and has damaging effects on werebeasts, vampires, and the dark ones. Supernatural creatures cannot hold gold without feeling the poisonous effects of the curse. A bullet dipped in gold will explode a supernatural creature's heart like a bomb. Gold against open skin has a searing effect.

grandmaster The master of a master vampire. Grandmasters are among the earth's most powerful creatures. Grandmasters can recognize whether the human he or she *turned* is a master upon creation. Grandmasters usually kill any master vampires they create to consume their power. Some choose to let the masters live until they become a threat, or until they've gained greater strength and therefore more consumable power.

Hag Hags, like witches, are born with their magic. They have a tendency for mischief and are as infamous for their instability as they are their power.

keep Beings a master vampire controls and is responsible for, such as those he or she has *turned* vampire, or a human he or she regularly feeds from. One master can acquire another's keep by destroying the master the keep belongs to.

Leader A pureblood werebeast in charge of delegating and planning attacks against the evils that threaten the earth.

Lesser witch Title given to a witch of weak power and who has not yet mastered control of her magic. Unlike their Superior counterparts, they aren't given talismans or staffs to amplify their magic because their control over their power is limited.

Lone A werebeast who doesn't belong to a clan, and therefore is not obligated to protect the earth from supernatural evil. Considered of lower class by those with clans.

master vampire A vampire with the ability to *turn* a human vampire. Upon their creation, masters are usually killed by their grandmaster for power. Masters are immune to fire and to sunlight born of magic, and typically carry tremendous power. Only a master or another lethal preternatural can kill a master vampire. If one master kills another, the surviving vampire acquires his or her power, wealth, and keep.

mate The being a werebeast will love and share a soul with for eternity.

Misericordia A plea for mercy in a duel.

moon sickness The werebeast equivalent of bloodlust. Brought on by a curse from a powerful enchantress. Causes excruciating pain. Attacks a werebeast's central nervous system, making the werebeast stronger and violent, and driving the werebeast to kill. No known cure exists.

mortem provocatio A fight to the death.

North American *Were* **Council** The governing body of *weres* in North America, led by a president and several council members.

potestatem bonum "The power of good." That which encloses the earth and keeps demons from remaining among the living.

Purebloods (aka *pures*) Werebeasts from generations of *were*-only family members. Considered royalty among werebeasts, they carry the responsibilities of their species. The mating between two purebloods is the only way to guarantee the conception of a *were* child.

rogue witch a witch without a coven. Must be accounted for as rogue witches tend to go one of two ways without a coven: dark or insane.

shape-shifter Evil, immortal creatures who can take any form. They are born witches, then spend years seeking innocents to sacrifice to a dark deity. When the deity deems the offerings sufficient, the witch casts a baneful spell to surrender his or her magic and humanity in exchange for immortality and the power of hell at their fingertips. Shape-shifters can command any form and are the deadliest and strongest of all mystical creatures.

Shift Celia's ability to break down her body into minute particles. Her gift allows her to travel beneath and across soil, concrete, and rock. Celia can also *shift* a limited number of beings. Disadvantages include not being able to breathe or see until she surfaces.

Skinwalkers Creatures spoken of in whispers and believed to be *weres* damned to hell for turning on their kind. A humanoid combination of animal and man that reeks of death, a *skinwalker* can manipulate the elements and subterranean arachnids. Considered impossible to kill.

solis natus magicae The proper term for sunlight born of magic, created by a wielder of spells. Considered "pure" light. Capable of destroying non-master vampires and demons. In large quantities may also kill shape-shifters. Renders the wielder helpless once fired.

Superior Witch A witch of tremendous power and magic who assumes a leadership role among the coven. Wears a talisman around her neck or carries staff with a precious stone at its center to help amplify her magic.

Surface Celia's ability to reemerge from a shift.

susceptor animae A being capable of taking one's soul, such as a vampire.

Trudhilde Radinka (aka *Destiny*) A female born once every century from the union of two witches who possesses rare talents and the aptitude to predict the future. Considered among the elite of the mystical world.

turn To transform a human into a werebeast or vampire. Werebeasts *turn* by piercing the heart of a human with their fangs and transferring a part of their essence. Vampires pierce through the skull and into the brain to transfer a taste of their magic. Werebeasts risk their lives during the *turning* process, as they are gifting a part of their souls. Should the transfer fail, both the werebeast and human die. Vampires risk nothing since they're not losing their souls, but rather taking another's and releasing it from the human's body.

vampire A being who consumes the blood of mortals to survive. Beautiful and alluring, vampires will never appear to age past thirty years. Vampires are immune to sunlight unless it is created by magic. They are also immune to objects of faith such as crucifixes. Vampires may be killed by the destruction of their hearts, decapitation, or fire. Master vampires or vampires several centuries old must have both their hearts and heads removed or their bodies completely destroyed.

vampire clans Families of vampires led by master vampires. Masters can control, communicate, and punish their keep through mental telepathy.

velum A veil conjured by magic.

virtutem lucis "The power of light." The goodness found within each mortal. That which combats the darkness.

Warrior A werebeast possessing profound skill or fighting ability. Only the elite among *weres* are granted the title of Warrior. Warriors are duty-bound to protect their Leaders and their Leaders' mates at all costs.

werebeast A supernatural predator with the ability to *change* from human to beast. Werebeasts are considered the Guardians of the Earth against mystical evil. Werebeasts will achieve their first *change* within six months to a year following birth. The younger they are when they first *change,* the more powerful they will be. Werebeasts also possess the ability to heal their wounds. They can live until the first full moon following their one hundredth birthday. Werebeasts may be killed by destruction of their hearts, decapitation, or if their bodies are completely destroyed. The only time a *were* can partially *change* is when he or she attempts to *turn* a human. A *turned* human will achieve his or her first *change* by the next full moon.

witch A being born with the power to wield magic. They worship the earth and nature. Pure witches will not take part in blood sacrifices. They cultivate the land to grow plants for their potions and use staffs and talismans to amplify their magic. To cross a witch is to feel the collective wrath of her coven.

witch fire Orange flames encased by magic, used to assassinate an enemy. Witch fire explodes like multiple grenades when the intended victim nears the spell. Flames will continue to burn until the target has been eliminated.

zombie Typically human bodies raised from the dead by a necromancer witch. It's illegal to raise or keep a zombie and is among the deadliest sins in the supernatural world. Their diet consists of other dead things such as roadkill and decaying animals.

Photo by Kate Gledhill of Kate Gledhill Photography

Cecy Robson (also writing as Rosalina San Tiago for the app Hooked) is an author of contemporary romance, young adult adventure, and award-winning urban fantasy. A double RITA® 2016 finalist for Once Pure and Once Kissed, and a published author of more than twenty novels, you can typically find Cecy on her laptop writing her stories or stumbling blindly in search of caffeine.

www.cecyrobson.com

Facebook.com/Cecy.Robson.Author

instagram.com/cecyrobsonauthor

twitter.com/cecyrobson

www.goodreads.com/goodreadscomCecyRobsonAuthor

For exclusive information and more, join my Newsletter!

http://eepurl.com/4ASmj

Made in the USA
San Bernardino, CA
29 December 2018